THE HOUSE OF JACKDAWS

Who is the stranger who comes out of the night of storm and lightning with raw and bleeding hands? He wears the name of Michael Grant on his stained, drenched olive-drab uniform. Castle Cormac has had many mysteries for Cordelia. She had been programmed for success in the Radio Therapeutic Department of a famous hospital, but finds herself clawed back to the House of Jackdaws — a kingdom, like Lear's, of intrigue and suspense.

Books by Alice Dwyer-Joyce
Published by The House of Ulverscroft:

THE MOONLIT WAY
THE DIAMOND CAGE
THE GINGERBREAD HOUSE
THE BANSHEE TIDE
FOR I HAVE LIVED TODAY
THE STROLLING PLAYERS
PRESCRIPTION FOR MELISSA
DANNY BOY
THE GLITTER-DUST
DOCTOR ROSS OF HARTON
THE STORM OF WRATH
THE PENNY BOX
THE RAINBOW GLASS
CRY THE SOFT RAIN
THE SWIFTEST EAGLE
THE CHIEFTAIN
GIBBET FEN

ALICE DWYER-JOYCE

THE HOUSE OF JACKDAWS

Complete and Unabridged

ULVERSCROFT
Leicester

First published in Great Britain in 1980 by
Robert Hale Limited
London

First Large Print Edition
published 2000
by arrangement with
Robert Hale Limited
London

Copyright © 1980 by Alice Dwyer-Joyce

British Library CIP Data

Dwyer-Joyce, Alice
  The house of jackdaws.—Large print ed.—
Ulverscroft large print series: mystery
1. Detective and mystery stories
2. Large type books
I. Title
823.9'14 [F]

ISBN 0–7089–4308–X

Published by
F. A. Thorpe (Publishing)
Anstey, Leicestershire

Set by Words & Graphics Ltd.
Anstey, Leicestershire
Printed and bound in Great Britain by
T. J. International Ltd., Padstow, Cornwall

This book is printed on acid-free paper

I dedicate this book to
Mrs. Bessie Jolley
my secretary,
without whose help in
typing and editing my manuscripts
I would have found life very difficult

JOHN JAMES BENEDICT CORMAC

m

CONSTANCE PEPPARD

GRACE	ROSEMARY LOUISE	CORDELIA (1)
M	M	M
HERBERT CRADDOCK	JAMES MACAULEY	WILLIAM KINSELLA
lived at	lived at	lived at
CASHEL FARM	LISMORE FARM	LYRE NA GREANA
(GONERIL)	(REGAN)	
		CORDELIA (2) (SISTER MARK)

Prologue

She stood on the very edge of a headland on the south coast of Ireland and looked out over the Atlantic Ocean. The gulls were wheeling round her head and there was cruelty in the yellow beaks of them, as they dived down to feather her face. At the last moment, they wheeled up and away and out on the thermals, graceful as ever, but fierce with the grace. There were nests in the long face of the cliff below, nests with eggs and nests with fledglings.

There had been a fisherman at the foot of the last climb and he had warned her against the gulls, but she had no fear of them. Her whole career had been aimed at the care of the sick and the dying, and the poor and the helpless. She was any Irish nurse at home on a holiday from England, dressed in a well-worn navy gaberdine coat, the belt pulled tight round her waist . . . the collar up, the blood-red lining of her hood, thrown back on her shoulders.

Yet here was no ordinary nurse. Here was a very extraordinary nurse indeed.

It seemed thousands of feet below her,

where the sea crept up the cliff like a grey slug. The waves crept up and up and then fell back again into the white foam of the breakers, as an insect might fall into cuckoo spit. It was a cruel sea, she thought. A full-crewed ship might run aground here and no sign of her to be found, only a few flung planks, that drifted in on the flow of the tide. They said you could hear the cries of drowned sailors sometimes, haunting the night. There was no softness here, no mercy. Here was all the hardness of nature, no loving tender care, and in that she had been groomed and coached and disciplined for the last few years.

The wind was freshening and there was a black cloud bar, coming up fast from the horizon. Soon it might rain and the darkness come down before the night, but she had no fine clothes to spoil, no fear of rain, only that the storm might come soon. She wore the blue dress of a sister under the coat, a trim belt, her name-plate on her left shoulder, that she was 'SISTER MARK', but that might mean anything. On her right shoulder swung the fob watch, with the sweep hand for the seconds, that might be life or death. She touched the watch with her hand, as if it were a talisman against the evil of this lonely place . . . tried to recapture the life, that might have been lost for ever. Then a great gull came screaming out of the sky, coming in on the wind and his beak slashing against her cheek. It made her step back quickly, hand to face with a smear of blood.

At the same time, the heavens opened and downpour of rain possessed the cliff top. The sky was as black as Good Friday, if ever there had been such a thing as Good Friday . . . and a temple veil rent in twain from the top to the bottom. There were times when she had doubts but always came the swift 'Mea culpa, mea culpa, mea maxima culpa'. Now the lightning jig-jagged across the top of the cliff, from zenith to horizon and the thunder crashed about her ears.

There was a mist stealing in from the sea . . . from the breakers and the thunder still crashing. There was no sight any more of the assault of the waters against the cliff base, only the white horses of Mannanan McLir, that rode the sea three miles out and on to the ends of the earth . . . on and on, and more of them and more . . . wind whipping them fiercely and the gulls back on their nests to look after their own.

Yet the girl did not seem to heed the storm. She was in some cocoon of her own thoughts, her hands thrust deep into her pockets. She had no care for the rain, that could make her dark hair, no darker. If there had been sun to shine, her hair could have been as iridescent as a raven's wing, a white straight parting to it and a clasp on the nape of her neck and a drenched pony-tail.

She had taken a wrong turn in life and she knew it. She was of high intelligence and had not thought fit to listen to the wisdom of others.

She should perhaps have listened, but that was not the way of it. She had chosen her own path. She had walked with her being full of sweetness and light, walked to within sight of the mist creeping up from the breakers. Now there were no waves against the shore any more, only the far-off white horses.

She had walked into a trap. Conscience was a hair shirt and she wore it with savage deliberation. It was in her training. Yet now, on the edge of a cliff, that had known shipwreck, not once, but many times, she loosed her anger against the Almighty. She met Him face to face maybe in the eye of the storm, as if she unleashed the dogs of war on Him.

'Are You really up there?' she demanded and her voice wasted on the wind. 'Or is it all a great confidence trick? Are we puppets on your string? Is death a sleep and a forgetting? I don't care, if that's the way of it. I'd like to sleep deep . . . not have to take the cruelty of life . . . but there's a belief in me, that I can't get shut of.'

There was a flash of lightning in her eyes and a roll of thunder straight after it, but here was a girl, who had never learned wise fear.

'Sometimes, I wonder what You're trying to do, God. You can't fool me, for I've lived it. I've seen the way You go on and You running the whole world. Don't You know that I've been in a position where I've seen You gather up little children . . . small and perfect in the flowering, just because You love little children? You've let them live, the badly formed ones. You've picked the finest for Yourself. Don't you ever think of the arms that are empty after them, empty and never to be filled any more? Why do You cast them untrue to your image and let them live on? Don't You recognize the breaking of human hearts? Is there any heavenly ruling in it all, or is it just a flick of the fingers . . . a cast of the dice?

The storm was in no way affected by her accusations and she faced God across the edge of the cliff and the almost continuing flashing of the lightning. Still, she spat into the face of her Creator, like a small hungry cat and wondered if the Devil would make a good advocate. More likely he would make away with her soul.

'You take the happy ones and You leave behind the misbegotten marriages. You take a man from his wife after twenty-thirty-forty years of marriage . . . Have You no knowledge that You're making her a half-person? What do You take from her and what do You take from his children? What does it do to her and to them?'

The thunder might intend to overwhelm her, but she rose above it.

'You let a teenage tramp discard her baby. Then You send Your glance raking the heavens for a loving married couple, who have never managed to achieve parenthood. Let them achieve conception and You flush this particular fertilized ovum down the sluice and maybe no more babies for him nor yet for her and a home unhappy. I've seen it. I know . . . '

She went a little way down the hill and the sun crept out from behind the thunderheads and all the small wild orchids made a carpet for her feet, but there was no thought in her head that anybody 'up there' maybe held her in high regard. She sat down on a grassy hillock and put her head in her hands, felt her hair drip rain down her back, under her coat . . . knew the feeling that a goose had maybe walked over her grave.

She was finished with her old way of life . . . the path of achievement, that stretched to the limit the work she did. Well she knew that the work was good, the way He had created the heavens and the earth, if that was anything to go by. She had done it by His law.

Now, she had been cast into a dustbin with slippery sides. She knew that an insect such as she herself, could never climb to escape. She had chosen her path, had insisted that she knew the way, but she had not counted on the slippery sides. Quite suddenly she had found herself in the House of Jackdaws.

'There's no future for you there,' the Devil had whispered, 'Get the hell out. The tiles are dropping like autumn leaves. There's no tea left in the caddy this minute. There's no cash in the till — and it's not as if there's anything left to build on now. Full well you know it, you, a highly trained sister . . . best there is, and you've been had for a fool. Pack your bags and get out. The Jackdaws will take it all over in the finish, whatever you do. I promise you . . . and you've tried. Nobody will ever be able to say that you haven't tried . . . '

'The Jackdaws,' the girl thought as she got to her feet again. It's true that the estate *was* good enough, but it had gone down and down and there was no power on earth could ever haul it up again . . . not after the last disaster. You might grow mushrooms under the floors, but there was no future in that, when they grew free in the fields of County Cork in the right season. It was just a matter of waiting the time of the year and you could come back from a walk with your hat full of mushrooms — and running over.

The storm was beginning to lift and the headland was a carpet of diamonds and through the carpet of diamonds, the small many coloured orchids still glowed . . .

The nurse was slight, of average height, as graceful as the girl, who walked through the fair with every man's eye upon her. Yet, she recognized the jackdaw quality in herself. They were social birds, jackdaws, and they flocked together. They tumbled through the skies and dived and twisted and turned and brought jocularity into the seriousness of the rooks, returning to their roosts for the night. In time, they would take over the old house, the jackdaws, and she considered herself no better than they. When it goes to nest, the jackdaw finds any vertical cavity. There seems to be no sense in it, but the bird drops a twig down a funnel . . . a long stick to lodge sideways. At last, a stick will be caught and held and here is the basis for building, yet in some of these old houses, all the effort can end in a heap of twigs on a hearth . . . an armful of long sticks on a deserted hearth and a match to put to them to make the flame go roaring like a lion up the wide chimney and when the fire was dead, nothing but the wide deserted hearth again, and a few grey ashes.

The girl had come to know that her life had turned from what might have been success to failure. It had no more value than an armful of starting sticks in a wide chimney hearth and echoes in the house and maybe the cawing of the jackdaws, but that was small comfort. They would have to build another day, and that was their habit.

She thought herself the greatest jackdaw fool of all time and smiled a little crookedly. Her teeth worried her lip at the thought of the slugging, slogging work she had done, week after weary week, to build a place high in the echelon of nursing. Loving tender care, it was to be, this thing called the nursing of the dying, but it could all come to a hearth empty but for the tumbled heap of catching sticks and at last the small grey dust, when the fire was gone out for ever.

Yet she turned at the foot of the rise and ran her hand through her soaked hair. The sky was lightening and the storm looked as if it might pass over. There was a pink at the lower edge of the clouds and the evening star was out and now you could hear the murmuring of the sea, because the wind had veered to the south.

'Why don't You watch what goes on down here?' she asked God and wondered if she did not deserve a spear sent through the floor of heaven for her impudence. 'Why don't You see that things run smoothly an odd while? Surely it's time You did? It's Your creation after all. It's Your responsibility, when one comes to think of it . . . and You can't say I didn't try. Oh, my God! How I tried.'

★ ★ ★

Then she shrank down into herself . . . knew pride and the sin of it, yet there was defiance in her still, though she crossed herself against harm as the Lady of Shallot might have done.

She smiled as she remembered the evening when the Superior had interviewed her in that august study and had advised her to try to curb her pride and her imagination, yet the Superior had painted God as an elderly gentleman in a white nightshirt and with a long white beard . . . a most benevolent man, who might put you through it, and would, almost certainly, forgive you in the finish.

Of course, He would never be a benevolent kindly old man. He would be sharp and big-business to match the year and the time and the way things had changed. Maybe he might wear clerical grey, just for the look of it, but there would certainly be a touch of Savile Row. She could see God now behind His executive desk and that would be top Chippendale and of course, He would look at her over the top of rimless glasses.

'Maybe I'll consider giving you some backing, Sister Mark, but you do realize that you'll have to produce collateral. I don't bet on losers. *Maybe* I used to, but I've given it up recently. After all, a person has to help themselves and you've lost badly this time. You might think of taking out a mortgage, but then there's percentage. I wonder if you've ever really thought seriously of helping yourself for a change? I'll send an Agent to see you . . . see what's to be done, but I'm getting weary of being taken for granted. We'll see what transpires, but frankly . . . '

She laughed and stretched her arms out to the evening star and thought that the Superior had been right about imagination, yet her black mood was gone and it was going to be a clear night. It was time she got back to the House of Jackdaws, that was Cormac's

11

Castle. There was a rumble of thunder, that chased her down the first valley.

'Why don't you do something about it yourself, Cordelia Kinsella?' God had asked her . . . and that was that . . .

1

I remember . . . I remember . . .

I remember the house, where I was born and where I lived for what seemed a whole lifetime. It had been a tenant farm of Cormac's Castle and my mother had received it as her dowry, when she married my father. It was never a very prosperous place, but it had a beautiful name, for they called it Lyre na Greana, the river branch of the sun. Coming on summer, the sun brought out the wild strawberries along the banks, where the wild primroses had grown and there were hazel nut groves to harvest in autumn, and before that, cowslips in plenty to make dodge balls, after the primroses were over . . . and the whole place was rich in blackberries and red rowan berries and over all, the gorse reigned, never out of blossom . . . the symbol of immortal love, and the sun . . . it was never done shining.

It was not a prosperous place, rich only in beauty. It was unsurpassed for loveliness, but loveliness does not breed money and John James Benedict Cormac knew that full well.

Yet I was born and brought up in what was a reflex of heaven and if I were to be born again, I would choose Lyre na Greana, the river branch of the sun. Till the day I die, I will remember the sweetness of it . . . will remember the love of my mother, Cordelia Kinsella, who protected me from all harm, but I know it was never a prosperous place, not in terms of agricultural produce . . . of cattle, sheep and pigs . . . only maybe in dreams . . . and maybe Cordelia, my mother, never had any dreams come true, but to look down that path sears my soul and I cannot take it, but hide my eyes against the cruel thing that a man can be . . . a man, who thinks that he is all powerful . . .

Cordelia . . . her name was apt enough and I bear it too and am proud of it, but it was strange the way it turned out. Cordelia! Cordelia! She had level pegging with the Virgin Mary in my eyes . . . still has the same rating now, when the story's told.

But I must begin at the beginning and go on to the end and get some order into it.

My grandfather, John James Benedict Cormac lived in a castle in grey history out near the cliffs of the Atlantic. His wife had been Constance Peppard of Strawberry Hill, She was 'gentry' and it had seemed to her family that she had married beneath herself

14

to wed Cormac of Cormac's Castle. She had breeding and education and he had a family tree, growing back down the ages of Ireland. She had wit, my grandmother, rest her soul . . . wit till the day she died. It was she who renamed her daughters Regan, Goneril and Cordelia, but Cordelia had been truly christened Cordelia and I was to be so named. Somehow, I think she saw it all before it happened and knew the folly of her 'King Lear', my grandfather . . . and mighty proud because he had caged him a peacock. He was a stubborn man, oh! yes, he was a stubborn man and well she knew it. He had taken it into his head to cancel out his estate duties and he in no way near the time to be making a will. It was all to save tax and he thought himself a shrewd man, did King Lear. He had the bit between his teeth. There was no turning him. As she told me herself later, he was not half old enough to die, when he took the final dividing of his lands. He decided to spread his wealth between his three daughters and he owned Castle Cormac in Munster and a number of tenant farms. He had called a family conference.

'It's no good throwing away money to the government. They would take it all off a man these days, if they could.'

So he had brought them all together in his

castle and grandmother looking at him and knowing how little wisdom he had, but loving him just the same.

So here were Goneril and Regan and Cordelia and their affianced men and a big hospitality put on for them to arrange the dowries before the weddings, but their names were Grace and Rosemary Louise and Cordelia Cormac, the daughters of Castle Cormac. After the table had been cleared, they came to the business. Maybe Cormac had never heard of King Lear, but he re-enacted the start of it.

'How much do you value me . . . my elder born speak first?'

That's how Shakespeare has it, but no doubt it was not exactly like that in Cormac's mouth.

Shakespeare has it that Goneril replies that she loves him 'more than words can wield the matter . . . dearer than eyesight, space and liberty . . . beyond what can be valued, rich and rare . . . no less than life' . . . and so on and so on and so on. Then it is Regan's turn 'I find she names my very deed of love only she comes too short, that I profess myself an enemy to all other joys with the most precious square of sense possessed and find I am above felicitation in your dear highness' love . . . '

Of course, it was not like that at all . . . only in a great outpouring of affection for their father and much of it false, as they proved to the hilt later . . . and my mother, Cordelia was sickened by her sisters, maybe said to herself as Cordelia does in Lear.

'What do I do? Love and be silent?'

It happened the same. It was my mother's turn and she was Cordelia, and truly she bore the name and her father pressing her to outbid the others for his love, but she would have none of it.

'I love your majesty according to my love . . . no more no less' but then she would not have used Shakespeare's words.

She told him plainly that she loved him as much as any girl loved her father, but soon she would have a husband, she must love him more. If she had a child, that child would have the best of all her love and there might come a day, when she had a daughter, Cordelia, named after herself . . . and that was indeed to be myself . . . and she would love that child better than the whole world . . .

John James Benedict Cormac had taken drink that night, but that was a usual state with him and he proceeded to destroy his life, as many a man had done.

'You're saying that you'll love an unborn

brat and a daughter at that, more than you love your own father? Who's to say that any of you will spawn children at all, and if you do, you'll be running to me for hand-outs for the whole tribe of them . . . '

In older days, Cordelia, the youngest daughter of King Lear, had been cut off from her inheritance and Lear's wealth left split into two portions between the two fulsome daughters, but in my family version, Cordelia had not been totally cut off. There was this little farm called Lyre na Greana — the river branch of the sun, that Constance Peppard owned and she had held her will strong for once against her husband's. If Cordelia were turned empty away and if all the Castle farms were to be divided up between the two elder daughters, then Cordelia, her ewe lamb, should have Lyre na Greana outright this very day . . .

'Lismore Farm to Regan then and Cashel Farm to Goneril, but of course, he called them by their right names. He had looked across at Cordelia and his scowl fierce, for Innish Bawn Farm was to have been hers, the best of the three.

'Nothing to you, Miss. I'll tear Innish Bawn down the middle and half to each of your sisters . . . teach you to watch your tongue, but you'll never learn anything only the hard way, so your sisters will live off the fat of my property. Go beyond to Lyre na Greana this very day like your mother says. There's no welcome in my heart for you to make a laugh about a daughter's love for anything but her father . . . even to mentioning a child that's not even thought of, yet and maybe will never be. Nothing to you from me! Make the most you can out of your mother's inheritance, you and your man Kinsella. 'Twill grow a grand harvest of gorse and brambles, but you can't live on gorse and brambles nor yet a basket of hazel nuts nor an armful of berried rowan branches. You'll have turf to burn, but you'll have no pony to cart home the cut peat . . . for if I'm disinheriting you this minute, I have a mind to do it properly. I'll find a way to make a mark on that smile of yours. I'll show you the cost of ingratitude and defiance . . . '

'And maybe honesty, Father?' she said.

Maybe Constance Peppard had whispered against her daughter's ear that he would soon change his mind, but he was as stubborn as a mule and so was my mother. It was all a gigantic storm that brewed up in a family tea-cup. My aunts had leapt on the disputed Innish Bawn and their men wasted no time in appointing a legal man. He stamped their claims and Innish Bawn was theirs . . . and my mother was married to William Kinsella and went to my grandmother's Lyre na Greana and that was where I was born when the months had gone by . . . at the river branch of the sun.

So Regan and Goneril had gained rich dowries and my grandfather had trusted them to see after him in his old age, but old age was not yet. These were modern days and a man must avoid death duty as best he can or go beggared. Cormac knew, or thought he knew, that he could trust his two loving daughters. He tried to write my mother out of his heart . . . so time passed and I was born in Lyre na Greana, in the river branch of the sun, and looking back on those days, I am quite sure that the sun was always shining and the white clouds sailing across blue skies . . . and the pools in the peat land reflecting the stars when the evening was coming down, so that you could almost put out a finger and touch a star . . . take it in the hollow of your hand to make a wish. I was a happy child and all my days were happy.

The other heinous crime my grandfather had committed, was swept out of sight and never mentioned before my ears . . . only sometimes I wondered at the sadness, that possessed my mother. I was to hear about it much later, but just for now, keep the legend of the dowering of Cormac Castle farms in the back of your mind, for it had big importance. The nub of it all was that the two elder sisters were barren and there was no heir for the castle. Cordelia had given birth to a daughter, myself, but if there was a feud on in the family, that only threw petrol on the flames. My mother was fertile — even if she had produced a child not a boy, as we say in Ireland. My aunts were barren.

To me Lyre na Greana was paradise. I remember . . . I remember . . . the kitchen with the great wood table, where we ate and where a great deal of the work was done. Particularly, I recall the horn-handled knives and the two-pronged forks to match them, the wooden egg cups, each with a brown-shelled new-laid egg, the thick blue-ringed Delft tea-cups and saucers, the cruet that had come from Cormac's Castle and had four separate containers for salt, pepper, mustard and vinegar . . . the pink bowl for fine sugar and a sifter silver spoon with it, the Irish soda bread, white and brown, and the fresh salt butter, new from the churning, the jam made from the September blackberries, maybe the crab-apple jelly from the wild crab tree in the hedge . . . and sometimes, butter-milk to drink or custard to slide down a throat, made from the beastings after the cow had calved. I remember the pancakes at Shrove and the barm brack at Hallowe'en, the turkey at Christmas and the plum pudding afterwards and the smell of the boiled pudding cloth like a washing day and the way the plum pudding itself was as round as a cannon ball and served with punch sauce. The open hearth burnt a Yule log at Christmas and we had holly and ivy up behind the pictures. I can look back down the years now and see my two socks fastened securely on the mantel-shelf and the small anxiety, that Father Christmas would have been and gone safely before my mother lit the kindling thorns under the log.

The work of the farm had to go on, but always there was a giant of a candle that burnt from the Eve of Christmas right through the holy night and on through St. Stephen's Night too. It shone from the other table at the window, where milk stood in earthenware vats for the cream to rise. It shone out across the yard, so that the beasts in the barn could get the value from it, Mother said, for all animals loved Christmas, as all children loved it, since the night that Christ had been born in a stable.

She worked very hard to try to make Lyre na Greana pay, Cordelia, my mother. She had hens for eggs, and eggs to hatch and to sell

. . . a cow or two. She worked as hard as any man in the hay-fields. She plucked and dressed the fowl and took them to sell in town on market days. She found time to make chocolates and candies and fudge, that sold for a good price, but sometimes, there was a hurried, harried look about her.

I heard an old man say one day that she had married a man with no work in him. It was in the square in the town and the old chap looked up at the bow window of the Hunt Club and saw Father sitting there, with a drink in his hand.

'Gentleman farmer, that boyo Mr. Will Kinsella!' he exclaimed and spurted tobacco juice into the dust of the street. 'He's so grand in himself that he'll hardly acknowledge his lady if he comes on her in the market with a basket of eggs on her arm, what harm, but she carries the whole place on her shoulders. If she hadn't that young lad, John Joe, to give her a hand, she'd never make ends meet.'

There was a general agreement about this between the cluster of men and another said that at any rate, Mister Kinsella was a grand ornament in the Hunt Club window.

'Himself will be in there beyond, giving out the pay on world politics and on farming and crops. Isn't he a great expert on keeping Miss

Flynn well exercised? She has her legs worn out trotting back and forth from the bar, sit in the window and chat to him . . . see to his comfort. He has his wife's heart broken, with one woman after another. I wonder what it is that makes Lyre na Greana's master a flame to the moths with the way they come chasing him?'

I was too young that day to understand what they were talking about, but I know it now . . . know that my father, Will Kinsella, was a man of straw, as poor a bargain as a husband for Cordelia, as Lyre na Greana had been, if you wanted a prosperous farm. Lyre na Greana had beauty, all the same, and peace and it was paradise for a child . . . this river branch of the sun.

It is important to get the picture of the family from the start.

Cormac's Castle was set out near the cliffs of the Atlantic, with my grandparents, and not enough capital left to run such a huge stone keep with its battlements that stretched for the sky. The three farms, that were now in control of my two aunts lay scattered across Munster. Aunt Regan had Lismore Farm and she went in for Jersey cows, made a go of them too, with her Walt Disney creations, bells round their necks to ring and their names on leather collars and their film-star eye lashes ... the automatic milking, the spotless shippons, the red rosettes from the Dublin Show pinned up in prominence of success and a pedigree bull at stud. Aunt Regan was what they call in Ireland 'a warm woman', but Uncle Regan was 'a poor thing', in the same parlance.

'Yes, dear,' he would say and Aunt Regan wearing the britches and that was no way to find married happiness. He kept an army of gin bottles under the stairs at Lismore Farm and childlike, aged eight, I had no tact. Aunt Regan's real name was Rosemary Louise Macauley but there's no point in remarking that.

'Why do you want to store so many bottles of gin, Aunt? Is it going to get inflated? And I heard one woman tell another the other day, that he's im-potent, but he has power hasn't he?'

I got a short answer and rightly so, for what business was it of mine, but after a few years the picture slotted into place.

Uncle Regan was drowsily happy. His wife was too busy to pay much attention to him and that day I thought it a pity, that she liked her famous herd far better than she liked her husband ... and of course, he had power.

As for Aunt Goneril, out at Cashel Farm, she had a fertile valley and she grew corn, barley, sugar beet and potatoes. You name it, she grew it . . . grew it better than anybody else. Of course, her name was not 'Goneril', but Grace, but Grandmother had called her that, and she had called her 'the ball of fire', and 'Goneril' stuck. I was terrified of her since the day when I had walked into her marital business.

'Why don't you and Uncle share the same bed, Auntie? Is that why you haven't had any babies?'

She stared at me for a long time and her eyes were as green as glass marbles with hate. Like a fool, I could not leave it at that.

'Anybody that's married shares a big bed. Mother told me it's more comfortable that way and one day she told me that's what the marriage service means by cherish. You cherish in a double bed, so she said and you should have a goose feather bed and lie very close together and your troubles are magicked away for you.'

'Are they indeed?' she asked me, her eyes frozen balls of ice now.

'Love, cherish and obey, you know,' I explained. 'Do you obey Uncle Herbert, for sometimes, it looks as if he obeyed you?'

'You're a foolish daft child,' she said crossly. 'He's the master of the house, not I. Cashel is a very fine farm and we've done very well for ourselves. If you do half as well, when you're grown up, you can thank Heaven, but I doubt if you'll ever amount to much out at Lyre na Greana. You can't make bricks without straw.'

Innish Bawn, the farm that was to be my mother's, they let off and it has no part in this story, only the rumour in the Province that 'it had the evil eye on it'. Still, it provided the two aunts with an income and it fed the other two farms into corpulence. Yet out at Cormac's Castle, there was now no sign of prosperity. There was no feeding in profits to Cormac and the castle was getting older and greyer and more neglected-looking and Cormac had leather-bound cuffs and elbows and the paint on the doors and windows, was shabby and there was an air of decay creeping into the fine estate, even when I was a little girl . . . little enough to be so tactless with Aunt Goneril, who was Grace Craddock, née Cormac.

Now and again, the two aunts came visiting Lyre na Greana, all dressed up and looking down their noses at Mother, because maybe they had caught her doing the milking herself.

'Isn't it high time Mark was trying her hand at the milking if you're so set on doing it for yourselves? Is it a dairy maid she's to be and maybe she'll try to outdo Cadbury's too. Chocolates made by Cordelia Cormac and daughter. That's a great come-down for a child of Cormac's Castle. We don't know where to look for the shame of it, but like mother, like daughter. I wonder you don't take up begging in the streets and done with it . . . '

The cold little sentences came out, one after the other and I could see Mother's cheek pressed against the flank of the black Kerry cow for comfort. I went over and stood beside her and put my hand on her shoulder to tell her not to mind them.

'Our father out at the castle isn't making any more great success than you are here, but he needn't come cadging help from us. He's got no help except himself and he had Mam's heart scalded with the way he flings the coin about. Isn't drink the curse of the country, the way they're all at it, your own man too, Cordelia Kinsella, lording it over at the Hunt Club . . . '

I cannot have been past eight, but I remembered the gin under the stairs. I looked at Aunt Regan without guile, asked her if the gin belonged to Uncle James Macauley and if he had it for a treat sometimes, like I had lemonade.

They were never on good terms, the

members of my family. There were times when one aunt might not be on speaking terms with the other and very often Cormac was not on any sort of terms with any of us. At Lyre na Greana, we kept ourselves to ourselves. John Joe came into the barn after the aunts had left that day to bring the cattle nuts and he saw that Mother was in low spirits.

'Don't mind what they say, Ma'am. You have the look of a princess about you, even if you are milking the cows.'

I knew well how to cheer her up. I had only to tell her that indeed she had the name of a princess too and I looked at her out of the corner of my eyes.

'I don't know why you had to call me Cordelia too,' I grumbled. 'Why couldn't you have given me a fine name like Dawn or June or Rosebud?'

'Well you're not bothered, for we never call you anything but Mark, because you're a sort of a 'Mark Two' person after me . . . and you take after me too. Besides, wouldn't you feel a right 'eejet' called Dawn or June or Rosebud, the day you turned eighty years of age?'

All the joy and the happiness was back in her laughter again.

'There would be people coming from every corner of the province to take one look at you, and that would be enough for them.'

She was never done seeing the funny side of life. Soon I was old enough to help her with the work. I sat on a three-legged stool and coaxed the milk down from the little Kerry cows and there were times, when the morning was so early, that I was half back in my sleep again, with the sping-sping-sping of the milk against the bottom of the zinc pail. I had to have my share of the work done before I set off for the National School in the next town and the aunts had plenty to say about that too. It was a great come-down for the grandchild of Cormac's Castle . . . direct blood of the Peppard's of Strawberry Hill. Things were going to the dogs and 'Jack was as good as his master . . . '

I liked school. I stayed after hours and picked up extra education. I read *King Lear* for myself and maybe I understood a bit of what went on. Was I not Cordelia, Mark Two and Cordelia Mark One saw to it that I sat at the cleared kitchen table at night and worked hard at my homework.

Then came my higher education, up in a college in Dublin, God pity her! Cordelia's hand-made chocolates, fit for Grafton Street or Bond Street, pointed me to the stars . . . I went across the sea and then up the sky like a shooting star. I had no thought that it was my duty to read agriculture and go home to the farm. There would always be somebody to run the farm and foot the turf, store the treasure safe against the winter, by the side of the house. I must go steeple-chasing along the race-course of the examinations, so that important pieces of paper might be delivered by post, professing this and that . . . Latin, Physics, Chemistry, English Language and English Literature too, French, History, Geography . . .

I loved my mother and I loved the farm, but somebody had blinded my eyes and put out my sight. My duty was there before me and me not seeing it, so I will know my sin of omission till the day I die . . . repent past the forgiving that I did not come back to Lyre na Greana and range myself at Mother's side.

'*Mea culpa! Mea culpa! Mea maxima culpa!*' and all without thought.

I said before that I had read *King Lear* at school. I knew of the hundred knights at arms, that Lear had demanded be kept for against a hard winter . . . a cut of pork, when a pig was killed . . . the small change of husbandry, but it did not work out, for Goneril and Regan had the money under their control and Lear was a beggar now and they had the power of what had been his money. The castle was falling to bits, but he got none of their bounty . . . not a sack of oats or a bale of straw . . . not even a quart of the Jersey milk. That I do know. They, who owed him everything, gave him nothing and he was too proud to open his mouth. Cormac had not kept enough working capital for his own estate and the castle got shabby and shabbier.

See me now, aged perhaps ten years, too old and too sophisticated to take Mother's hand . . . very ashamed of that too, going for a visit to Cormac's Castle and perhaps we did this once or twice a year . . . no more. Cormac still held it against Mother, that she had come to love others more than she loved him . . . and I, being her daughter, saw no

'CORMAC'S CASTLE'. It was enscrolled on the wrought-iron gates in gold paint, very fine and very proud. The estate ran on for three miles along the road on each side and it all belonged to my grandfather. Yet, it was almost barren of stock. Even I saw that. The drive was weedy and the woods on either side of it, had encroached on the roadway. Some of the trees had been chopped down and my mother was sad about that. Other trees had a painted cross on them and that meant that they were marked down for cutting.

'Doesn't he know it takes a hundred years to grow such trees and all to be screamed to their death under a chain saw in a few minutes?' said my mother.

'Here is murder indeed,' she said. 'They should not have let this happen. They promised. You know I can't help him much. I send him a few eggs and salt butter and pork, when we kill a pig, but what is that against the wealth of Lismore and Cashel? The poverty of Lyre na Greana breaks my heart. I send what I can, but it's not much, but there's no turning back time, and I'd have gone on my bended knees to him afterwards only for the other thing he did.'

I asked her what that was, but she said it was best that I knew nothing about it, and so we came to what I was always to call 'The

House of Jackdaws' . . .

Cormac's Castle might have been the palace of the High King of Ireland, give or take a few centuries. It was all leaded walks behind battlements and the roof slated. There were jackdaws that nested in the chimneys. The front steps wanted weeding. One or two windows had broken panes, and I thought of it as blind.

There was a butler to open the door, in a greenish black coat with tails and, the housekeeper was with him . . . Rose, who was his wife. The hall was an acre of stone slabs and Mother muttered that the floor wanted a good scrub. Other women worked under Rose's command, but they were not considered fit to appear in the dining-room. They hid outside doors and around gloomy corners and you might start them, as you would start a hare from its form . . . Medusa hair, tureen of soup in hand, downcast eyes.

I cornered such a person in the kitchen presently and she was very honoured, that I came down to thank her for the fine dinner.

'The place is going to hell on us, Miss Mark. There won't be a leaf of tea left in the caddy, after I've wet the pot this minute. It's all bits of driftwood, the bills coming in like they do on the shore below . . . and nothing to turn back the tide now. God knows I'd give my life for the Master or Herself, but lives don't shell out coin. Himself has no care that he's wasted it all away. He pours it out of the bottle into the glass and he's drinking away the bit that's left . . . the sheep and the cattle and the horses is all gone . . . the cocks of hay and the sacks of oats. If there's a hunt on, the gentlemen come in to eat and drink . . . all muddy from the chase . . . hungry and thirsty after the galloping and no care if there's no coin to foot the bill . . . and horses in the stables eating their heads off . . . saying Himself is the best host in the county . . . and the Mistress looking sideways at it all . . . and Claffey's bill to come in and it must be paid sometime . . . even if she sells the lovely gems she brought from Strawberry Hill, but they're all wasted now and sorrow on the day she wed him.'

Perhaps she did not realize that she was talking to a child, but perhaps I was old beyond my years.

'We'll have the bailiffs in for sure, Miss Mark, before we come to the end of it. We'll have no place to go for shelter, us poor old creatures. God have mercy on us all We've worked for the family all our days and always they were the roof over our head and the bread in our mouths against hunger . . . '

Grandfather had a kingly way about him. I

recognized his royalty, false though maybe it was, by the way he would greet me.

I must take wine with my dinner. I was wise enough to appreciate that he had denied himself none, for he was blurring his words.

'Burgundy goes with beef, Mark. White wine is for fish or boiled fowl, but a fowl's best young and broiled on a spit in front of the fire and maybe a fine claret to go with that. Champagne's all folly, good for weddings and birthdays. Give me a sparkling Burgundy, with 'beaded bubbles winking at the brim and purple stained mouth'. Your lady grandmother taught me that, but she knows such nonsense . . . '

He wandered into some world of his own presently and his hand sought mine.

'You shall have a dapple grey pony, Mark . . . the first pony I find, that looks like a galloper on a fair . . . long white mane and tail. You'll ride to cubs on St. Stephen's Day . . . I'll be damned if you don't.'

He murmured on and on and my grandmother took little heed of him.

'In three — four years, we'll have to look out a polo pony size bay with black points, or perhaps a chestnut. A lady's boot shows best against chestnut or grey. You'll be on the leading rein at first . . . no being frightened, but then a Cormac's never frightened. You'll not come down at the first double-bank. There's a knack to it that the Irish have. You'll have it too . . . just up and change feet and over.'

He took my shoulders between his hands and he stapled the words into my mind, with his earnestness.

'They say it's all finished, but it isn't. My children were all daughters and two barren out of three and no son, nor yet a grandson and won't be . . . only a child, a girl and that's yourself, Mark. What's in a name? There's a torch in Cormac's Castle for the carrying . . . but two out of three mares barren and only this fine-bred filly foal out of my loins . . . and my kingdom divided.'

He gave me a little shake and looked into my eyes.

'Your bones are like a bird's, Mark. Can they take a great burden? A thought came to me this minute, that one day, a great burden might be put upon these same shoulders of yours.'

I recognized the smell of the Christmas pudding whiskey sauce on his breath and thought how many of the family liked what they called the demon alcohol in the Temperance lectures at the National School. Someone had told us that drink put the devil into a man's mouth to steal away his brains and I wondered if that was happening to Cormac's family. Cormac had loosed me and had gone to stand at the window and look out on his fine lands.

'Cordelia was like Herself and the child is the dead spit of her mother . . . same name too and they have to call her Mark. There's a fool thing, but at least, she'll have a fine pony and she'll ride to hounds. I'll keep it in mind.'

I followed him over to the window and pulled at his coat, waited till he turned to look down at me. Then I explained to him that I had a jenny donkey, called Fanny, who was the same age as myself.

'She follows me round like a dog and I like her fine. If I get aniseed balls and hide them in my pocket, she'd follow me all the road to Dublin and back again. I couldn't be breaking her heart with taking in a fine pony and I have no time these days, with all the home-work from school in the evenings . . . '

Then my grandmama decided that there had been enough conversation in front of a child and came over to break it up. She walked with a slight limp on an ebony stick, but she said she did not need the stick if she could put her hand in my arm. She gave me the black, foreign magic-looking stick to hold and she told me it had come from Africa and it was supposed to have great power to heal the sick, but it had not done 'her screws' any good. She took Mother and me off to the drawing-room, which seemed to be a very fine place. There were deep velvet covered chairs and a velvet drape that ran on a rail behind the door. Over the marble fireplace was an immense mirror that made a little world of the whole room and there was velvet hanging from the mantel-shelf, that had a bobbled fringe on it, and I thought it the height of grandeur.

She showed me some albums of photographs and told me they were all family pictures and that I must look at them and know who they were. She led me to a table and told me to sit up straight. I was to look carefully through the books and soon she would come and tell me about the people who were in them.

'If they're forgotten by you, there's nobody to remember them. If you're not remembered, you're dead,' she said and that made me start off studying the elegant ladies on horseback and the ladies in bustles, the ladies in crinolines, the bearded men posed behind pedestals ... the pink-coated huntsman, though you couldn't see the pink colour because they were in black and white, and most of them browning with age.

There was a mouldy-age aroma to the big

Bible-like books and I felt if I had stepped back down a hundred years. Here was a fine turnout and a girl in it that might have been me. There was a big ivied mansion and a party, arranged on the front steps . . . and maids to wait on them with long white streamers to their white caps and their white aprons mottled with the mildew of the years. Here was one wedding, here another and a low voiced conversation between my grandmother and Cordelia, Mark One, at the fireside.

'It's so very good of you to bring the child to see us and I'm always breaking my heart for the foolishness that went on. If he threw our fortune to the winds, it was just because he was king of the castle and there was no advising him and holding him to reason. My own father is dead and gone this many's the long year, but I thank God on my knees, that he left me Lyre na Greana . . . left me enough independence to cry halt to disaster. I always loved Lyre na Greana . . . went there for a sweet honeymoon and played at nymphs and shepherds with Cormac. Then it was let to tenants and I used to wonder if the strawberries still grew wild in the grassy banks under the hedges and the violets and the primroses . . . and did the little waterfall make music by the side of the house all the year . . . and did you see a trout in the stream sometimes, but gorse taking it all over, because I had my honeymoon there and it was the time for kissing . . . '

I was startled by the poignancy in her voice and I glanced across and saw a tear running as slow as honey in winter down her face . . . so that I applied myself to the albums once more . . . and came on myself over and over again, down the past, aged about eighteen on a docked cob and once out in a governess cart with a very jolly woman, whom I did not know from Eve . . .

She came over to me presently, 'Miss Constance Peppard' and she filled me in on my ancestors and she told me that I must always be faithful . . . that it was better to die than to be disgraced and I must bear it in mind. She showed me a fine signet ring on her finger and that was written in Latin very small, in a crest . . . with *semper fidelis* and *malo mori quam foedari*, but I had a very little understanding of it, only promised her faithfully that I too would seek death before dishonour . . .

Then we had tea with small slices of bread buttered and rolled and with cakes fit for the fairies. She told me that I would never believe it, but the same cakes were made by 'the hen woman'. If you looked long enough, you could find what a person could do and the hen woman had 'a light hand', with pastry and cakes.

'And she'd have access to the eggs too,' I said very wise for ten. 'If she had plenty of eggs and beat them long enough, wouldn't any cake be glad to rise for her?'

She laughed at that and said I was a Daniel come to judgement . . . and we got along well together, but she was sad at parting from us. We walked away down the avenue and my mother very sad too, because she said the place was going to pot and there was nothing she could do about it. She was near enough to tears and she was so wrought up by emotion that perhaps she said things she would never have said otherwise. It was the aunts, who were to blame . . . but herself too. The aunts had promised to look after the estate in Cormac's old age. It might be true, he was not good at husbandry . . . God knows what I made of that . . . but they had promised to help the castle and they had not given 'the black under their nails' . . . had just picked quarrels and ignored the fact that the place wanted help . . . and they were living on the fat of the land themselves. Goneril had a mink coat for the Dublin Show and Goneril had a new car, that was so long, it could never go round corners . . . but she was no

wife, nor ever would be . . . and if I called
them by their proper names, she would take
an axe and kill me with her bare hands.

'My mother and their mother, nicknamed
Regan and Goneril. Let them stay Regan and
Goneril, till the day they die,' she said.

She could not make Lyre na Greana pay
enough to give any proper help. 'Your
father . . . ' she started and then stopped up
short out of loyalty.

'Maybe I started out to build up a
home-made chocolate empire, but I wasn't
much hand at that . . . never got beyond the
shops ten miles away and sweeties for the
farmer's wives, when I was thinking to sweep
the whole world, because they were good,
Mark. You'd not buy better home-made
chocolates, beyond in Bond Street, but I had
no advertising, no market for them, beyond
what was in an Irish country town. I've
broken my heart against it, but it wasn't to
be. I'll not stop trying. If I stop trying, it
would mean disgrace, and I'm a Peppard too,
just as you are. It will all work out in the
end . . . '

So the years slipped by and I had my own
world . . . school in the town and the extra
curricular activity after hours and at home
doing the home-work. I liked studying and
the information I picked up was like water

flooding desert land. I might learn 'I wandered lonely as a cloud, that floats on high o'er vales and hills', in class, beaten out on the anvil of a teacher's desk with the blackboard pointer, but after school, I came to know the most exquisite beauty in the full glory of its reading. I had hours after class, when a very excellent headmaster, opened my eyes and showed me Shakespeare and Milton . . . showed me that Latin was a language and that *Mensa, mensa, mensam* was not some strange barbaric rhythm, meaningless, but called 'the latin'.

I passed a scholarship into a school in England and my world opened like a pupil in a startled iris. I was up and away, with no looking back over my shoulder. My mother was pleased about my success and I had no thought to the fact that she might be lonely after me. Yet I deserted the farm and we packed my cases and I went, never turned my head to look back on the blue hills of Ireland . . . just thought the Sugar Loaf of County Wicklow, another hill, as the boat slipped out.

Back in the township, they were proud of me. 'Nothing was ever blind to her' they said and 'What's born in the bone comes out . . . ' 'She has it from the old grandmother,' they said and I adopted a proud tilt to my head, that maybe I had in no way earned. There was I, beyond in England, over the next years, first place and distinctions and honours flooding in like the swell of the sea and no thought in my head that my mother might be out milking the cows on a winter's night, fighting impossible odds and my father in the Hunt Club, an expert on world affairs, maybe taking Miss Flynn or one of new successors for a drive in the car. My rightful place was by her side. The boy, John Joe, grown to be a man, stayed faithful, but I did not, and therefore I wear a stripe . . . a yellow stripe down my soul, till the day I die, for I broke the family honour and did not realize it, thought nothing of it and knew myself fundamentally ignoble and will never think otherwise.

I chose the sciences. I was past 'O' level and on to 'A'. There was nothing to stop my success. I climbed up the teenage web like a quick spider, intent on making her mark. I was offered a university education and turned it down, because at last, it came to my mind that maybe I had no time to waste before I went to the help of Lyre na Greana. My mother looked a little wasted away, her eyes big and anxious. She had 'a lean and hungry look' . . . and there was not one item of luxury at home.

'Jesus! You'll have to do something about

this place, Miss Mark,' said John Joe. 'The mistress is killing herself and she's breaking her heart about Cormac's Castle and the master's no help in the slightest. He's away after . . . ' He stopped at that.

Over in England, I was taken to see the New Complex . . . the biggest, the best hospital in the world. Tomorrow there would certainly be a bigger and better hospital, but for today, here was Mecca. The Mecca of Aesculapius. It covered an enormous area of good agricultural ground and the builders would never be finished with it, or so it seemed. There were always scaffoldings and vans and lorries and 'MEN AT WORK' notices and British workmen, with famous names advertised on their backs of their overalls, 'McAlpines Army'.

There were high-rise buildings, that touched the clouds. There were corridors in every direction on every floor, so that a patient could get lost between one department and the next. There were glass windows instead of walls and the sun took turns to be kind or cruel.

Here was a hive of industry of ill-health. It was big business too, grown up like Jack's Bean in the pantomine and perhaps the complex, the greatest pantomine of them all.

Patients crept along the walls of the

corridors like old grey rats, confused, disoriented, greatly awed, thinking that 'oh! deary, deary, deary me, but this was none of I!' There was nobody to ask the way, no time to care. The lifts shuttled up and down from one floor to the next and the next and back down to the lowest floor of all, to the dreaded basement, but that was the end of life, with its filing-cabinet of death.

Outside the buildings, were the compounds, where the coloured car-beetles parked, and ex-service men, who ruled with the power of the Hitler they had conquered. There were nurses, who spun between one department and another, almost dead with tiredness at the end of a shift, dishevelled and disoriented and with job satisfaction wearing mighty thin.

The ambulances were white or blue and some of them were 'routine' and some of them were 'accident' and some of them were 'red alert'. Some of them were in no hurry in the world, ferrying non-ambulant patients to and from long-booked appointments. Many of the vehicles had strident voices, that reminded the old people of the air-raid sirens, but that was long ago now.

It was big drama, the new complex. You could lean down and pick up any part of it and weave high drama out of it, for here people lived and here people died and from here the cars fetched out the living and the hearses fetched out the dead.

The Radio-Therapeutic Department was the magnet that drew me from the first day I went there. It had been forgotten and left behind at the old site, though technically it was part of the new complex. The old hospital was virtually empty now and the wards might echo with memories, but Radio-therapy was a gallant ship, that still sailed on and perhaps Nelson had the telescope to his blind eye . . . and Nelson was 'the Proff'.

I had trained as an S.R.N. at the new site and I wore the black belt that meant far more than being a Judo Expert. It meant that I had been chosen to be one of our own hospital's nurses and presently I was moved over to Radio-therapy and became a sister and up and up the ladder I climbed.

I still went home to Lyre na Greana for leave, but always the Department drew me back to Wentbridge. Perhaps I might not have deserted Ireland for Accident or Surgical or Medical or Orthopaedic, but 'R.T.C.' was special. It had charisma. It had 'the Proff', as the best captain in the world and it had a crew, who caught dedication from him. It had a passenger list of dying patients, and just the odd few who came out in victory.

'He's so kind,' they said. 'He draws up a chair and sits by the bed and he talks to them . . . nothing too much trouble for him.'

It was quite a miracle, how the whole department caught flame from his fire. The patients might be sick unto death, but it was rare to see anything but a smiling face . . . and such kindness was out of fashion nowadays. You met a stranger in a corridor and you smiled . . . and the stranger smiled.

So I was very happy and rather proud to have become a sister in Radio-therapy. The beginning of the day in hospital was not just another getting up to milk the Kerry cows. Here, was any famous hospital, the night staff gone off and the ward rounds beginning. In a room, long and narrow, as an Irish country chapel, the chairs would be set for pews and a table for an altar at the top. The room would have been filling for fifteen minutes by twos and by threes, new probationers, student nurses, medical students, post-graduates — house-officers, along the seats at the sides, and sub-consultant staff. Then at the moment the clock hand moved to nine, the door would open and 'the Proff' would be there, his two registrars at his heels. There was always a look about the house-men of worry, of being too sleepless at night and of being worked off their feet. It was the cost one paid for becoming a consultant, but that complexion of being too much indoors and having all work and no play was becoming the facies of medicine at the end of the ninety-seventies.

Radio-Therapeutic-Department . . . it was a top that hummed about 'the Proff', but there was a basic humanity about him . . . a humility that made nothing of his world fame. He had the sad face of a jester and always he wore a careless suit of dark clerical grey . . .

The ward sisters moved in like proud galleons, each in her special uniform, that were colours on a mast . . . the starched caps of St. Thomas's, of Guy's, of Bart's, of Wentbridge itself and each with a proud set to it. They held an armful of case-histories. They sat by 'the Proff' and one by one they produced the progress of each individual person under care. Diagnosis, treatment, prognosis and all the small change of the individual patient in that particular ward . . .

The senior registrar would start at the beginning and describe all the details of the admission, go on to give the information from so many tests. Then the X-rays would be produced and slotted into the lit panels that ran along the wall at the front of the room.

'Now let's put the original picture beside

the films taken yesterday. See how the cloud in the sky, no bigger than a man's hand has spread to here and here and here. Poor Mrs. Free! We'll see her in the ward presently and maybe you'll remember the speed of sarcoma in a young woman . . . '

He would turn to Sister Goode and ask her if Mrs. Free's appetite was any better.

'What did she have for breakfast this morning, Sister?'

How could a nurse remember one in forty breakfasts?

'Cream crackers and butter and Marmite and a glass of sherry. You said to try the spicy appetizing things and it worked well.'

'Poor lady! She will never hanker any more for her newspaper of fish and chips, nor her steak and kidney pudding . . . all the glory of eating. The glory of eating is departed and perhaps some of the student nurses could tell us what that symptom is called?'

'Anorexia, sir.'

'The Proff' looked as if he were laden with the sorrows of the cross.

'One can ask how do we make her fat and jolly again, able to do two men's work in the sugar beet fields on a cold winter's day, with a sack for an apron. The answer is that we can in no way do it, *not yet* . . . but one day, one day . . . '

The years slid away and perhaps I worked as hard as any woman on the sugar beet harvest in the Fens. There were so many new techniques and this was a teaching hospital. You had to keep a perfection in your ward, maintain a happiness and a sense of getting better . . . a throwing of dust of mercy into eyes and also the easing of pain. There must be an enormous amount of happiness, with no cause for happiness whatever. Always the banner was HOPE. The R.T.C. staff were companions . . . good companions. The rest of the hospital called us 'the British Navy' and that was praise indeed. I gained more and more experience and came closer to 'the Proff'. Then all at once, I was his senior sister, when I had thought at one time never to attain 'S.R.N.'

'Good morning, Sister Mark,' he would say to me at the beginning of each day. 'Come and sit by me and tell me all the loads you've raised from my shoulders today. I never met such a colleague for shuffling out trouble before it starts . . . and if you're going to start an argument about all the gin we're using for the Brompton Cocktail, don't open your mouth. Heroin, cocaine and gin, as much as is necessary for the relief of pain, and that's it. None of the modern men have concocted anything better. Brompton claims it was their formula. In the Edwardian days, they made do with *pil.opii*, one grain and the chemist rolled them in gold and dispensed them in a small round box. Think of it . . . a lie in a small round box and 'One to be taken as often as necessary for the relief of pain' . . . '

The world of Lyre na Greana was completely divorced from the hospital. It might have belonged to another planet and 'the Proff' knew all about it, for he had encouraged me to talk about it to his wife and to him. Sometimes, I put down my problems at their feet as a dog might put down a flung stick. Mrs. 'Proff' was a lady doctor, whom he loved, as no Anthony had loved his Cleopatra . . . She made the cherishing of him her life's work . . . craved no fine career other than that . . . they asked me to supper sometimes, encouraged me to talk.

I loved my holidays in Ireland. I could still milk cows. It was like riding a bicycle, 'Mrs. Proff' said. You never lost the knack of it, and I was soothed with the ping-ping-ping of the milk against the bottom of the pail in the dark of a morning and wondered why I did not give up all my fine career and go home where I belonged. The butter milk was bitter-sweet to my tongue, the best cure for thirst in the world. The salt butter on soda bread, with honey from the comb was better than all the exotic dishes of the world . . . the bacon boiled with drumhead cabbage in a pot served with potatoes thrown on top of the stove to brown to crispness — or maybe potatoes creamed and mixed with white cabbage and that was called Colcannon and sometimes, there was a ring in it, to say who would be married first . . . and it was all joy and home and my own flesh and blood. Time was made for slaves and there was no hurry but to stop and talk or just to stand and stare. Then after two weeks or maybe three, back would come that feeling that I wanted to be up and away and Mother would sigh and her face might seem lonely and lost and white, but I had blind eyes and now I knew that Father would have some girl in tow, for he went from one to the next, like a bee and sipped what nectar he could, but there was no industry in him. I saw him still in the Hunt Club window, with Miss Flynn trotting after him from the bar, but he had progressed from those days and I was the last person to know. My mother kept her own counsel as she did about a great many things. God have mercy on her! She never even told me about the white mare . . .

I had gone back to the hospital one time, not even observant enough to see that she was fighting a last losing battle. They found her at the kitchen table with a perfect batch of chocolates set out before her, ready for the shops the next day, the violet crisps and the rose chips, the rich pink cream and the rich violet cream . . .

I stood at the graveside and threw the small posy of flowers down on the coffin, judged myself and condemned myself . . . sentenced myself to my duty, for as long as I should live.

I entertained the aunts and their husbands the Craddocks, the Macauleys, to funeral meats and there was bitterness in my mouth afterwards, for they ate as much as they could and came back for second helpings, cocked their ears at the reading of the will and advised me to find a good man and get married, before 'I was too long in the tooth' . . .

'The farm's not worth a thraneen. It's mortgaged to the hilt. Will Kinsella will have to shake the laziness out of himself and roll up his shirt sleeves. He's not going to be a kept man any longer . . . '

In a kind of nightmare, I noticed that he had three or four women hanging on his every wish and it was obvious that they were waiting to take Mother's place. I took the night train out after the position became clear to me, that it was finished. There was no place for me here and nobody wanted me.

They were all glad to see me go. My father said bravely that he could manage and that John Joe could see to the farm. The train taking me out from the platform ran back down the years and at last, I knew how it felt to be really alone. I was pointed towards Wentbridge and the starched cap . . . towards the comradeship and the loving tender care.

'There is nothing you could have done, Sister,' 'the Proff' said gently, and 'Mrs. Proff' put her hand over mine.

'There's no point in giving up your career at this stage. It was the way it worked out. Don't expect to put on the wisdom of Socrates at your time of life, as if it were a warm coat. There are no warm coats. Haven't you learned that yet? Just let the time go past. It will soon seem better. We can fill your life past flooding in R.T.C. with the people of despair.'

'But not the one . . . not the one I loved.'

The 'Proff' smiled his jester's smile.

'Just rest tranquil here for a year or two. Put it out of your head that you didn't do your duty. By and by, you'll see the whole picture. You'll see what went on and understand.'

I plunged into my work to the exclusion of all thoughts of self-guilt. Within nine months, Father had married again. I was not expected to attend. They knew that I would be too busy to get leave. 'Kitty' had moved in as a housekeeper and she had thought it wise to 'regularize the friendship'. From Aunt Regan came a virulent letter . . . 'To think of a woman of such morals moving into her dear sister's home and I was to be sure of one thing, if my father had a son by Kitty, he would be no blood relationship to Cormac's Castle. I need not worry about losing my heritage. Lyre na Greana might be left to a step-brother, but the castle was entailed to its own people . . . '

Aunt Goneril was disgusted with the whole affair. My father should have had more consideration for the rest of us. The girl was 'of the lower orders' and all her attraction was in sex and there was that about the whole tone of the writing that made me wonder in sudden intuition if Goneril had no use for sex. Suddenly I remembered bits of overheard conversation . . . things that had meant nothing to me in my childhood and I thought a jigsaw might have slotted a picture. Goneril's whole life was Cashel Farm. She slept apart from her husband . . . likely she was frigid. Regan's man was impotent. Somebody had said that years ago. By now, I knew this did not mean that he was without power. It explained the unhappiness in the house and the bottles of gin under the stairs, the drowsy indolence of Regan's husband and the general unhappiness that hung over the whole family . . . and no heir to Cormac's Castle. It was all nonsense. I put it out of my mind. Well I recognized that we were a most peculiar family, but had not King Lear's family been strange too and the Galsworthys and the Barretts of Wimpole Street?

There was very little correspondence between Ireland and myself. It was as if the islands had drifted apart. We sent cards at Christmas and perhaps a letter then. I could never face 'The river branch of the sun' with Kitty, its mistress. I saw Cordelia, my mother, still there in the dark of the mornings, sitting on the stool, with her cheek against the black-haired side of the little Kerry cow and almost I seemed to hear the milk ping-ping-ping against the bottom of the zinc pail, and her laughter.

I heard from my grandmother fairly regularly with news of Cormac and his castle and I wrote back to her. Maybe once in three months a letter passed between us and she always signed it 'affectionately yours'. I think she did have an affection for me and she wrote a newsy letter that kept me in touch with Cashel and Lismore, with more than a trace of humour in it. They were talking, her daughters, or maybe they were not talking.

'They really should put up some sort of a sign, so that people know, Mark. It can be very embarrassing in conversation, when one farm does not recognize that another exists. Then the next time one sees them, they are in each other's arms, because 'Jersey Lily' has taken first at the Dublin Show . . .

'Your grandfather is getting vaguer than ever. He sat down in a chair the other day and intended to take off his glasses . . . took his dentures out instead. He wanders upstairs to change for supper and appears down in his nightshirt, ready for bed . . .

'Old age diminishes us towards childhood and I find myself remembering my childhood far better than the new things that happened yesterday . . . but I can see beyond the mountains and not what's in front of my nose . . . and give my love to yourself . . . and your love to me. We don't forget you at home . . . '

So the years slid by till the day came, when 'the Proff' sent for me to come to his room and his face serious. We were old friends by this. I set about producing a cup of the Cona coffee he liked, and we watched the water filter up and away and up again and I had a carton of cream, in some magical way, because we all spoiled him. I poured it down across the back of a spoon and smiled at him and it was just another difficulty to be solved. Solved it would be . . .

'There's a medical man in the South of Ireland, Mark, who has written to me about you. Perhaps you've heard that things are going badly in Cormac's Castle. Have the aunts written to you?'

I shook my head.

'Your grandmother is ill and the castle is finished. They had a conference with the family about what must be done. This doctor chap was candid about the aunts. They suddenly remembered, that there was a nurse in the family, when conveniently, they had forgotten your existence for years. They both think it's your duty to go home . . . I rang the doctor . . . spoke to him at length about the whole set-up. I got the story out of him.'

He looked across at me sadly.

'Your grandfather seems to have put great faith in you . . . different stuff from your two sisters. He might be glad to have you at home to look after the lady, your grandmother, but I'd have you know that there's no facility of any kind in Cormac's Castle for home nursing. This doctor wants his patient admitted to a hospital and she won't go. It's the usual social problem with a very difficult family set-up . . . difficult as they come. They've decided to pin the duty to you, as a qualified nurse and God help all qualified nurses, for the family burdens they're asked to carry!'

He looked at me glumly and told me that I was a bigger fool than Lear, if I put a foot in Ireland.

'You owe them nothing. You owe the family nothing. Your two aunts could cope with the situation and after all they had their share of inheritance, while your mother was fobbed off with Lyre na Greana. They've never done anything for you and neither has Lear. My God! Your two aunts don't even visit the castle any more . . . '

'My grandmother and I were friends. She never cast me off. We wrote letters and she's a fine person with a sense of humour . . . '

'The local doctor sent some advice to you. I put him in the picture about you and told him what you had to come . . . success and success and more success. I told him that you were a key figure in the department and that I could not replace you. He told me to tell you from him that it was his considered opinion that you should stay where you are. You've built up something here and you've done it by yourself. Don't let them crucify you with their cries of 'duty',' he said . . . 'When the duty is theirs.'

'The Proff' took my hand in his and told

me that the one person, that had helped me was in her grave, and he meant Mother, but I hardly listened to what he said. I knew the answer was 'yes' and not 'no'. I could never live with a 'no'. I had only to think of Constance Peppard's loving letters and her apologies about the dappled grey pony. I had only to think of the wad of pound notes that Lear had thrust into Cordelia's hand that day and how she had paid it out to the publican at the cross roads. It was an old situation in classic literature and it always ended in tragedy, but one had to walk up the steps.

'If you want to save yourself, Mark, run away from it.'

'Proff's' voice was very sad and the jester face was tragedy.

'I have a dreadful feeling that you'll never come back to us any more and we'll be the losers. If you want a career, don't go now, but knowing you, you're on your way.'

He put his head in his hands on the desk.

'A hundred people will miss your kind hands. You'll be throwing away your God-given talents, but go over to that Gothic castle, if you must. Come back to me if you can, when you learn disillusionment with mankind.'

'I must go. You know I must.'

'I knew your answer, before you gave it. I

had a strange feeling that this will be your last morning on the rounds. I know full well you can take no other action, you being you. Just for now, know there will always be a place here . . . and maybe, you'd like to see Lear's letter? You made your decision before you read it. Maybe your grandfather knew you better then any of us, and that includes yourself . . . '

So I read the letter and I caught the next train out of Euston and I travelled the Irish Sea and went down across Ireland by the fast express. I made the last bit of the journey in a carriage that had a cattle van and a guard's van and was still drawn by a steam locomotive and so I came home. There was nobody to meet me on the windy platform and I left my cases and walked out along the country road with just a small night bag. It had been perhaps fifteen years, since I had stood at the wrought-iron gates of Cormac's Castle, three miles from the station. The name was picked out in gold still, but there was no splendour about it. The hinges were worn and the gates must be lifted back and the avenue had grass growing along the middle of it and the trees meeting overhead in a deep tunnel of green. The blackberry bushes were rampant and the elder trees and all the rhododendrons run to trees, for the want of cutting back. There were nettles and thistles and neglect had put its ugly stamp on the place . . . and the thorn trees had run as wild, as if they encircled a sleeping beauty's palace. It might stay undisturbed for a hundred years. I wondered idly if I were the one appointed to set it free and then laughed at my own vanity and the avenue turned and twisted, till it shot me out on the place before the front steps . . . front steps all grass between the stones and the white door running green down the paint . . . the knocker green with not being polished . . . and slates from the roof down in the drive and never replaced . . . and the windows blind in places . . . not polished for a long, long time. In the old days, the maids had shone the glass on Tuesday and Friday and the knocker was polished every day and the stones were free of weeds and grass and no weeds in the drive either, or so I recalled, but my eyes had been child's eyes, overawed by the grand thing it was, to come to Castle Cormac.

The same man answered the door to me now, but he had dwindled down and the acre of hall had grown smaller. I got a flash back of memory to the dining-room table from many years past. There had been that long polished spread of mahogany and the silver and the glass, with such a shine to it . . . and the china, that maybe did not match, but was very fine indeed. I remembered the candlesticks of silver and the candles that burned with softness and how my grandmother had told me that all ladies were beautiful in candlelight. The decanters were jewels of topaz and ruby and diamond. The soup had been cold, but it did not matter. The fowl was superb and the vegetables were fresh from the garden. There had been a chocolate pudding just to please 'Cordelia's girl' and that was myself, and I could taste the hot chocolate sauce in my mouth tonight and see the steam rising from the richness. It had been in the shape of a hare and Lear had given me a sip of Cockburn after the dinner and said 'the child must learn' and he had made a great fuss about me and told me that I was well equal to two grandsons . . .

'You'll inherit what's left of it, Mark. I like that name. You'll see that the port is still passed round the table clockwise direction and that you pick the walnuts in the paddock tree for dessert. It's your fingers, that will be brown from the picking of the walnuts in thirty years.'

And again, 'Mark, my little one, you know the value of one young Jenny donkey and love for her, against a dozen fine grey ponies, against a hundred men at arms and all their horses . . . that pride of horse! You're the lassie for me. There's no doubt in my mind . . . '

I had read the letter, Cormac had written to the Professor . . . my mind made up before I read it.

'I have wondered if somewhere there is not one person, who can raise the castle like phoenix from its own flames. Tell Mark from me that here is nursing for a stout heart. God pity us! There's an empire here still, as potentially great as Rome or Greece. I liked that little girl though rarely I saw her and she had a faithful heart among all the treachery . . . Cordelia's girl. How I want help now and Cordelia gone, but she's Cordelia come back again in some miracle. I have no right to beg for her help . . . to bring her to a fallen fortress. I think there is that in her eyes, that might lift us up again to the victory . . . might put it together again from nothing . . . with nothing left . . . might undo what I did with my own hand. I've brought the Jenny donkey from Lyre na Greana. God only knows why, as if I bought a bait to bribe her child self again to visit Castle Cormac. The donkey is the only beast in the stable and she's hungry, this ass called Fanny, hungry for a lump of sugar from Mark's hand. I even coaxed John

Joe to come here to work and willingly he came, for love of that little girl, but maybe she's forgotten all about the sugar in her pocket . . . '

The devil thoughts! There were slates off the roof. One of the battlements had crashed into the drive. The whole castle was falling to ruin and blindness in some of the windows.

The butler, O'Brien, and his wife were a little old man and woman on a weather house and perhaps she came out if the sun shone and he came out if it rained.

'There was sorrow on us when Miss Cordelia's husband married again,' she murmured. 'A beast would have mourned longer.'

It was strange to hear a native Irish woman speak in Shakespeare's tongue. Almost I expected her to go on with the bit about the shoes not worn with which somebody or another had followed 'my poor father's body' . . . and that was from *Hamlet*. Yet there was no 'river branch in the sun' for me in Lyre na Greana any more. I thought again of Cormac's letter . . .

'I don't want to vampire young blood. I ask the help for my lady. I cannot care for her properly any longer and I am sorry to have to come, cap in hand, to beg, but my darling does not want to go into hospital to die by herself . . . '

The bell pull had come away in my hand and I threw it away into the shrubbery and old O'Brien retrieved it and promised that he would repair it and put it back and it would be as good as new in the morning. Before it died, the bell had had a deep funereal note. Yet now, these two old people stood side by side, their faces lit with gladness at the sight of me.

O'Brien was full of concern.

'Go upstairs now with Rose. She has a copper jug of hot water for you and a hot jar in your bed. Maybe you'd lie down a while after the journey, before you go in to see the mistress, but you'll find her sadly changed from the old days.'

His face was a withered apple and there was a tear, that ran slowly, as clear as a drop of dew on his cheek.

'If you were to know what a relief it is to have you standing here and you a fine lady grown. We've done what we could but time's slipping away. We had nobody to tell us what to do for the best. The days ran out like the sand through a glass . . . '

They had blankets pinned across my grandmother's windows to keep the cold out, but the air too. There was no fire in the

68

grate. The bed was freshly made, with far too few pillows. There was no bed tray . . . no jacket for her shoulders, only one of her old hand-knitted cardigans and it wanted washing.

Her hair was unkempt and the diamonds gone from her fingers. Her face held all the delicacy of the last stage of death, the same ethereal beauty . . . and a plait of white hair, lying along each shoulder. God! Here was a picture I knew well by now. Here was a job I could do and no turning away from it. I had been just as tired on the wards a hundred times and for some reason, I had changed into my uniform before I went to her room. Her face accepted me as the State Registered nurse. She could have no knowledge of the Senior Sister of Radio-Therapy . . . no idea of what power and glory I had left to come to her, but there was no importance to that now. My thoughts ran round in my head like mice . . .

Tomorrow I would start to see what could be done about the total decay of Lear's Castle. They had put down basins and buckets and bowls to catch the dripping leaks from the roof. There was moth and rust and surely decay. The house was dying with the old lady . . . Miss Constance Peppard of Strawberry Hill.

'So you decided to come?' she demanded brusquely and no smile on her face, only a look that took me in from top to toe.

I smiled at her and went into the old routine of loving tender care and it was second nature by this. I went through the familiar drill of general nursing. She was on the edge of sleep, before I had done. I had not seen such pride in a woman's face for a long time and it was with surprise, that I saw the pride was for myself.

'You've spoiled that fine linen apron making up a coal fire in the grate, but you knew the comfort it would be to my heart. My father used to say a coal fire was all 'Bugle eagles and trillily eagles and silver spoons and tatthers', like brillig and the slithy toves, you know. He made it up for me and I aged four, sitting with my feet in the hearth. There was more to it but I can't recall it now . . . 'silver spoons with smoke handles and blue tatthers', but it's gone, like everything else.'

There was a sigh as light as the fall of ash from the fire.

'You're a good gel. I thank ye . . . and I like that starched cap of yours and the starched band under your chin. It's been hard-gained, that cap you wear, as proud as a queen's crown. It suits you fine . . . '

The next moment she was asleep and I turned down the light and the fire sharpened her face and turned the ceiling to shadows.

Quite suddenly, beyond all shadow of doubt, I knew I had come home. This was the place I was meant to be . . . here was where I belonged.

2

Don't walk away

My grandmother painted the complete picture of Castle Cormac for me, as she lay in bed with the blankets down from the windows and the coal fire bright behind the bars . . . and herself propped up on six pillows, to rest just so . . . a milking stool for a cradle over her feet, for there was nothing else. There were flowers for her eyes and cologne for her hands. I had found the lemon verbena bush and brought in a spray for her pleasure. I laid a last dewy rose against her cheek and she sighed.

Through the days and sometimes through the nights, when she was restless, she talked and I listened and I heard what I had only half known through my childhood, the story of King Lear, was set to a new pattern and now I was to hear it, in pieces and in snatches, from somebody, who had seen it played out.

'The gels had picked their men . . . indifferent men. There was to be a dowry for each gel. Himself set the deeds of the three farms of the Cormac estate in front of him on the table . . . Lismore, Cashel and Innish Bawn . . . fine properties, all of them. He was tired after a day at hounds. I recall the brush of mud on his cheek and the gels sent for, but he looked very fine in the pink coat. When he laughed that evening, his laugh echoed up into the gallery, but it proved no cause for laughter with what went on. It was all such a joke to him and when he was like that, no power on earth could stop him . . . no more than a baby could stop a runaway horse. It was like a game to him. The decision of the disposal of his property was to be made on how much his daughters loved him and he with a glass in his hand and no knowing where to stop. Goneril and Regan were bees after the honey pot, but Cordelia didn't like it. She came to sit over beside me and my hand in hers. Regan went to sit on his lap like a child, the foolish gel . . . great grown lumpish woman! Goneril was saying she'd never love her future husband, as she loved her pa . . . better than she loved the whole lot of us and that included me, her own mother. I'd have boxed her ears for her, but I held back.

'They knew what was going on, the two eldest ones. They knew Lismore was the richest farm in Munster and they were both after it like terriers after a rat. Regan said she'd die for him, wound her arms round his neck and a deal of foolish talk out of her. Cordelia saw that I was worried. She knew that Cormac could in no way give away capital so lavishly. He was putting himself at his daughters' mercy . . . trusting them to see after him in his old age. She never moved from my side and her hand tight in mine . . . '

Maybe an hour passed in the dim light of the fire, before I heard the rest of it, but I made no effort to prompt her. At last, she spoke.

'Then it was Cordelia's turn.

'You're my father,' she said. 'I love you as much as any girl loves her father, perhaps a maximum, but I love Mother too. I love my chosen husband. I'll love my children, when they come. I love this place . . . always will. I love practically everybody in the world. It's a super world . . . '

'She gave a little laugh then and tried to make fun of it.

' 'I've been thinking just now and I got a guilty conviction that I love 'Bawn', better than the universe itself, but you gave her to me.'

' 'Bawn!' he demanded and again 'Bawn!?'

' 'The grey mare you gave me, pa. Do you know that she follows me round the stable yard like a dog? If I sit on the gate, she pushes her nose into my back and fires me off into the paddock. She demands an apple or a bit of bread roll as her right after dinner. Sometimes, I sit up on the gate with my back to her and pretend I don't know she's there'.'

'Bawn' is spelt 'Ban' in Ireland and it means 'white' . . . and a white horse is called a 'grey' properly. A grey is a grey and when it gets old, unlike the rest of us, it is still a grey, but now came another pause. My patient was not asleep, just away in the past. I made up the fire with apple logs and the smoke smelt sweetly. Then after a bit, the tired voice went on.

'It was one of these family tiffs that blew up into a tornado, from nothing. He was aggressive with drink and it was as if Cordelia came on the fire of his anger and threw oil on it.

' 'You know what 'Bawn' means to me, Pa. She's the best present, I ever had in all my life.'

' 'But to sit there and say you love an animal better than you love your own father? You're an unnatural child, but you've always been the same. If I was going into town and asked you what I'd bring home to you, you'd tell me to bring myself safe to you. At least your sisters could tell me they wanted a box of candies or a handful of ribbons, but you had to be after something fancy, and it was just for effect. You wanted sweeties too, and too proud to ask for them, so you'd have myself safe home, knowing well, that that would draw richness out of me, because I'd think you cared for me most, but it won't wash this time.'

'He took the deeds of Innish Bawn in his hands and he tore them in two, threw half down before Goneril and half before Regan.

' 'There's a postscript to your dowry, lassies. Cordelia shall go hungry. You'll divide her portion between the two of you . . . and let her learn what it is not to be the daughter of a rich man.'

' 'I'd be rich if only I had the Colleen Bawn,' she teased him, but she did not mean to anger him, only to say what his gift had meant to her and he chose to take it the other way and I got up and went out of the room and I found my desk and the deeds to Lyre na Greana. I could not bear to see her so mortified. I gave her the deeds of Lyre na Greana . . . into her hand . . . told her it was to be hers and she could be independent of her dowry from Cormac . . . and maybe I pushed the whole thing into open war.

'She told me she loved me, but that I must not tear myself into two halves.

76

' 'I'll get by, ma,' she smiled. 'I'll still have the Colleen Bawn and her hair will be white too .. with time, for all the dapple grey she is today. If I have the Colleen Bawn, I'll never despair no matter what time does to me.'

' 'Then I'll take her back from you.'

'He told her to go and see how she'd fare if she tried to take the mare off the estate.

' 'There's no welcome for you at Castle Cormac any more, my lady. You'll go upstairs now and you'll pack your traps. You'll get off my property and you'll not put a foot on it again. I'm king in my own castle. Your sisters will see me want for nothing, because I've looked after them tonight. You can go and see how hard it is to make your own way, for at this minute, you're not worth a farthing. You're a 'penniless lass with a lang pedigree'. That'll take you a very short distance' . . . '

Here was history I had never heard before and the words so soft, that I had to stoop my ear to her mouth.

'The mare was a half Arab. Your mother treasured her over heaven and earth and the beast worshipped her. She'd go riding without saddle and bridle, guiding the animal with her knees pressed into the flanks . . . both of them attuned to freedom. They were perfection in movement, just one person, trusting the other completely . . . and

Cormac gave the mare away . . . sold her beyond to England, with no thought what might happen and the whole affair conducted in secrecy and shame, so that there was no tracing what had gone on. It was an act of the cruellest spite I ever saw. I did what I could, but perhaps I made things worse that night. I left the room with no word and I got out my desk. I had found the deeds of Lyre na Greana. It was a thing of very little account, but it had been my dowry, when I married. I went back to the room downstairs, but I told you that, didn't I? and things were worse not better, for the other two girls were out to make trouble . . . and Himself the Lord of Creation still. I wanted to stop loving him for what he had done, but I'll not stop loving him till they put me in the burial plot on the hill . . . maybe not then, aye, maybe after that, my heart will beat again, if he stands by my grave . . . '

There came an hour of sleep from the heroin mixture. Then she was drowsily awake and the matter of my mother still on her mind.

'Cordelia, your mother was right to refuse the grey pony that day for you . . . even if Cormac was trying to retrieve his soul for what he did. I owned Lyre na Greana. I could give it outright to your mother there and

then, just to get the lost look out of her eyes
. . . no, not you . . . to Cordelia, your mother.
Sometimes, I cannot distinguish one of you
from the other, but the stuff takes away the
pain and somtimes, I think that perhaps I'll
get well, but I've been so happy since you
came back to me . . . and Cordelia was
banished to Lyre na Greana and the mare
was sent across to England and I could find
no trace of her, though I looked, but there
was a conspiracy of silence . . . and horses
were being shipped to the Continent for
butcher's meat . . . and I hoped that she was
too fine a beast to be taken away in a
deathship, but how could I be sure? Nobody
dared talk about the Colleen Bawn, vanished
between one day and the next and her
mistress, your mother, banished from the
castle too . . . and such a feud started, that
went on down the years and made a deal of
bitterness . . . so that it turned into a family
of evil and unhappiness and distrust and
greed and loss of faith and love . . . and all
those trifling little meannesses . . . and one
not talking to another and the marriages all
gone sour . . . and no laughing or lilting at the
break of day, when a man turns to his wife's
arms and there's heaven for them, just to lean
out and take . . . and find paradise in love
. . . and fulfilment . . . only one filly foal and

that was yourself, there in the middle of a vortex of hatred, but sometimes, not often, your mother brought you to visit and it broke my heart, because you were my baby over again . . . and the same honesty in you, the way you turned down Lear's fine pony that day for your own Jenny donkey . . . and ye'll never know how I loved ye for it . . . ye're herself all over again and she in her grave . . . the same loving eyes and gentle hands . . . the same pride, that would never give up against adversity.'

One night she was wandering and near enough to the end to see into the next world, from where she lay.

'I found Cordelia crying in the saddle room. She had gone to Bawn's loose-box. It's still there at the end of the big barn. She left that stable for Bawn to come home to. She left the saddle and the bridle and the horse blanket all set out. She said goodbye to me and she walked along the avenue with her head held high on her way to Lyre na Greana . . . and her man had no courage in front of Lear, to come and walk at her side. We sent her possessions on in a farm cart . . . Himself did not come to her wedding. He was a 'foolish fond old man' even that day . . . and the folly was his own doing . . . and down the days, the story was told in sorrow. She had

Lyre na Greana and her young husband. She was happy then, or I think she was, though there was no richness with it, and she was a lassie, that had been used to being waited upon. Then you were born and she was happy indeed, only that she could never find 'Bawn' . . . '

Another night and the small hours and she restless, finding herself back in the past.

'I married against my parents' wishes, you know, my dear. I had made my bed and I must lie on it. They never acknowledged me any more, the Peppards . . . 'married to that barbarian out at Cormac's Castle'. They paid me off with a peasant's farm and they wanted no more of me. I had Lear and I could make what I liked of him. Besides Cordelia had Lyre na Greana, and she made it paradise . . . at least I thought she did. Then I wondered. She came to see us sometimes and you'd think nothing had happened, by the way Himself went on with the little child . . . that was yourself. You never even saw me except as an old lady, with diamonds on my dirty hands and the establishment starting its sliding fall. The diamonds were all sold, but they could not stop the famine for money. Even the roof's leaking now . . . and Regan and Goneril . . . how aptly I nicknamed them, for they were false . . . false . . . false

. . . They did not know . . . never wanted to know. We were a hill-billy family in the mid-west. There was no good to come out of them . . . only a petty mean, bickering jealousy of Cordelia, because she had conceived a child . . . '

Then one of the last nights of all and the end at hand . . .

'Sister Mark, I'm glad to have known you and to have loved you . . . to know that my Cordelia will never be dead, while you live on . . . to know I've had a chance to tell you what went on . . . to know you've had the whole truth . . . to try to thank you for the way you gave up your proud career, for my poor self.'

I had got her room into some semblance of comfort in a nursing unit, for a gallant lady on her way through to the night, I found linen sheets in the cupboards and embroidered tray-cloths, that probably dated back to Strawberry Hill. I rifled the cupboards for delicate china. I whipped up dainty meals. Always there was a small sprig of flowers on the bed tray. There were sheepskin rugs that went under her poor back. There was an Irish woven carpet of great beauty . . . fit for the President himself. There were silver candlesticks, just for the polishing and petit point pictures, put away and forgotten.

She fretted about the tiles on the roof, for there was no safety for Himself under a broken roof. The slates were off, but they were lying in the long grass . . . and the grass wanted cutting too . . . I must ring up and get a man to come.

'Damp will destroy any fortress . . . like strong drink . . . and bitterness.'

'It will never destroy your fortress,' I said.

I cornered John Joe, whom I knew from childhood and now he lived at Castle Cormac, having been brought from Lyre na Greana.

'It should not be beyond our capability to lay slates, John Joe,' I started. 'Take a look in the grass and collect as many as you can. Mix a bit of cement for . . . '

'Why will you never give up, when you know you're beaten, Miss Mark? The ladder is rotten with worm.'

'I'm not afraid of heights,' I said. 'And anybody could lay slates . . . '

He found a great many good slates, just for the picking up. He mixed the cement. He was still doubtful about the ladders, but I went up them like a spider, thinking it best not to give them too long to take the weight. It was a wonderful view out over the Atlantic Ocean from the roof of Cormac's Castle and I stood there and prayed St. Jude, the patron saint of hopeless cases, to let the ladders take the weight of John Joe too. He showed me how to lay the slates. I laid the slates. We made the roof secure again. We went down safely and took away all the buckets, basins, and bowls, and John Joe said it showed that I had great faith in our work.

'I had faith in Saint Jude too,' I told him. 'And it was a grand view over the ocean.'

John Joe said he hoped the same ocean would not take the whole roof off, come the first gale.

I had stood up there, looking out over the battlements, towards where I thought the hospital must lie and had asked myself how I had ever come to such a place.

I worked part-time builder's labourer and part-time sister, but although I might slow the death of the castle, I could not halt death itself. It went on for a long time. The roof was sound. It was a chance to patch up the big barn. There was timber for the cutting and bracken for roofing. We had no credit in the town, so we pulled out old nails, to use again.

At first, I had tried to contact Regan or Goneril, and I make no apology for continuing to identify them by those names. It seemed that communications had been cut off or virtually so. The telephone was unanswered in both houses. If I called at the actual farms, I was told that the mistress was not at home.

'Besides, she can't be upset by what's going on at the castle. It's Himself's own fault. He's made his bed and Herself says he must lie on it, even if he's filled it with nails.'

At Regan's farm, the woman was a conspirator. She drew me into the kitchen and gave me two dozen eggs and a pound of Jersey butter.

'Don't let on I gave them to you, but I know what went on.'

I stumbled down the back steps, hiding the food under my Sister's cloak. Who was I to be proud? Those eggs would make fluffy omelettes for Lear's wife and the butter go well on small fingers of toast. John Joe wolfed down six fried eggs and he ate home-made bread with fresh butter, told me that we had the barn nearly done and that the animals would be as glad of it, as he was of the fried eggs.

Constance Peppard confessed that it was a weight off her mind that the man had been to make the roof sound and the big barn safe against the winter. It made her feel like Robinson Crusoe and she knew there was no worry any more and could go to sleep happy . . .

I hope that she died, thinking that we were on the way up again. Death was merciful to her, as it can be the odd time. She might have had to fight a longer harder battle. As it was, she never lost her beautiful fragility, her Dresden-china look, the brightness in her blue eyes. She was gone between one minute and the next, after the tiny omelette and a Minton cup of tea.

She asked for the mirror, the brush, the comb and I loved her for the way she faced up to the inevitable.

She made her 'vale', as if she knew the time had come.

'I'm grateful for what you've done, Mark. Like Oliver Twist, I'm asking for more . . . and shamed of myself. When I'm gone, would you see to Himself for me? He's not without blame, but then, who is? He was a man of straw, just the same, as the ones my daughters chose, but my children are blood of his blood too. I was never able to stop loving him . . . foolish, fond, old man . . . '

She seemed to be speaking to her reflection in the glass.

'There's an enchanted thicket sprung up round his castle. One day a person will come with the years, maybe has come. I've thought . . . It will all be as it used to be. Perhaps it's too late, but you tell me the roof's good again. Could you find it in your heart not to go . . . when I'm gone. Give him a little more time, just because of the way I love him, no matter what he did, to your mother . . . my daughter.'

She laid the mirror down gently and the brush and comb tidily beside it, reached out and took my hand, grasped it tightly and I thought of how my mother had gone that night, to hold her hand.

'I might have done it myself . . . gone back down a hundred years and turned the swine out on the fallow land. They'd have ploughed and made it fertile and you can sow potatoes the next year. It was the way food was grown in the old days. John Joe is young and strong, but he hasn't the head for planning. You have . . . '

Her hair was fresh washed and her eyes were like aquamarines.

'I won't run away from Castle Cormac,' I promised and saw her pride in me.

Then I saw terror take over, but it was gone in a flash and she fell sideways on the pillows, her eyes open and the pupils deep and still, a trickle of blood at the side of her mouth . . . now the tears pooling in the corners of her lids . . .

I plaited the hair down each shoulder and went into all the routine of the terminal drill and a nurse must never weep, but I found myself weeping now.

There was nothing for me at Castle Cormac with Constance Peppard dead. It was a sinking ship. I must see to the funeral and then get on my way. At least I was leaving the Place far better than I had found it. Lear could go to perdition in his own way. He was the cause of every piece of misfortune, that had happened on the estate. I must save myself. Lear had taken away the white mare and he deserved hell for that. It was Elizabeth Barrett Browning and Flush all over again. Positively I disliked Cormac and he had never been particularly civil to me, since the day I arrived, I had had no invitation to stay.

They were moving Radio-Therapy out to the new complex. They were installing the most modern equipment in the United Kingdom. They wanted me back as never before. The scope was enormous and I must be Head of the Nursing section.

Just for now, I would stay on here . . . make no move to go, till the funeral was over and she lay at rest, only I knew that she would never be at rest, if I deserted her now. I had promised to stay. I remembered with a sinking heart, what I had said in the last minute of her life . . .

'I won't run away from Castle Cormac.'

I had promised faithfully and there was no walking away from it. As I thought about it, the Jenny donkey called out three times from the paddock below the window, as if she accused me of betrayal . . . like the cock, that accused St. Peter . . . and who did I think I was?

'You loved me,' said Fanny, the donkey. 'Cormac had me brought over from Lyre na Greana and John Joe too. They all had faith in you. They all said you'd bring peace back to this place. Hee-Haw! Hee-Haw! Hee-Haw! Don't say you're going to deny and desert, *Sister* Mark!'

So the cortège left the front steps and Cormac was destroyed entirely, seeing nothing, feeling nothing, understanding nothing. He had not moved from his seat by her bed, since she had died and the decanter still full beside him and he not touching a drop . . . cold, stone sober, so many years too late, so very many years . . . and time never to be turned back.

'For pity's sake, don't leave me, Mark. I cannot live without her . . . I'm selfish to ask you for more time. Just stay with me through a few black weeks. She wanted the place risen up to its old grandeur, the way it was, when she came as a bride. The other day, she told me that she could see into the future, but she was full of the draught you gave her for the pain. God bless you! 'Take it,' you said. 'If a wineglass of it doesn't help, take another. Pain will never find dominion over it . . . hasn't done for a great many years now'.'

He gave a deep sigh and said that I had seen to it that Herself had had 'a happy death'. Then he went on.

'I remember the day I promised you a hobby horse pony, but your mother was an honest woman. She shelled out my money to the man at the cross-roads to settle for a part of what I owed. You told me you had the donkey at Lyre na Greana. A while ago, I bought her from your father . . . coaxed John Joe to come here to work. John Joe and I have put our heads together . . . planned to make the castle a kind of monument to Herself, but we could never do it on our own. We could never do it. I've given up the drinking and that's a start. If we could plan how to go on, we could build it up again for the love of Herself. Aye, for the love of Herself. We might do it . . . '

His voice died for want of hope.

'John Joe and you and I . . . and Rose and O'Brien . . . '

There was a faint fire in him like blown turf ashes and I prayed that the decanter might stay full, but the funeral undid all his fine intentions. The family turned up in full force and they stood like vultures round the grave in smart black. As for me, I wore the pride of my sister's uniform, with the red lining of my cape a banner . . . with the starched white cap some strange token of pride . . .

I have only to glance back down the years to see the hall again and the funeral over and one of the aunts at my grandfather's side, keeping his whiskey glass refilled, splashing it over at the brim, down on the mahogany table.

'God rest our lovely mother! Our hearts are broken with her loss, but it's no good your getting ideas in your head, Mark. If the whole place were to be auctioned, maybe, it would clear what's owed. The old man is full of dreams and visions, but it's just not on . . . '

They went away at last and I tried to plan some future. John Joe and I had put Himself to bed and we went downstairs and found O'Brien and Rose, disconsolate in front of the big black range. I was still wearing my uniform and maybe the cap was the last pride I had left.

'The ladies was right all the same, but they shouldn't have come out with it like that,' Rose said. 'If the whole property is auctioned, maybe the debts might get 'ped', but I've known the day, when this place was the pride of Munster and the three little daughters, running around it like three princesses and nothing too good for them ... and the two eldest ones promised they'd see after Himself and they should think shame, it's come to this. It was a wild thing he did to put faith in them and he only middle age. It was a bad day, when he spread out the wedding portions, for he put a curse on the place and things never went right, not after that little white mare left the stable, for she carried all the luck of the castle with her and it rained on the hay and corn green in the stooks ... and the beasts took sick of nothing and died on us. It was as if a thicket had grown round the castle and evil in it ... and that evil might stay with us, till the spell was broke in a hundred years, like in the fairy books.'

I got a shivering down my back, that maybe I was that person. My grandmother had hinted as much, but it was a rôle, that I in no way wanted. I tried to remember what she had said and had it 'A person would come down the years'. I am nothing if not superstitious, but, how could I quit on a losing battle? I was so tired that my thoughts jumbled in tangled wool. Was it worth a try? There were the O'Briens. There was John Joe. There was myself. We had a few cows ... a few derelict sheds and one fairly good barn now.

I took the Waterford glass of whiskey that O'Brien held out to me and drained it in one long draught. It burned me up with fire.

There was bracken for roofing. There was timber for the felling. There was the transport of Jenny donkey and her cart. There were goats wandering the lands and they could be rounded up. Goat's milk was good for delicate children . . . allergic children could sometimes drink nothing else.

We had little or no money, but a few trees might be sold. Trees could buy concrete and there was a quarry of sand.

John Joe took the round plate off the top of the stove and shoved in a handful of kindling and a few logs, some pieces of turf. O'Brien had my glass half full again.

'I might get some agency nursing in the town,' I said. 'We'd have to have money coming in.'

'We have a clamp of potatoes against famine,' Rose whispered. 'We could live on potatoes and milk and eggs from the hens and milk . . . '

'We could buy cockerels, day old and rear them . . . sell them for the eating. We'd get by,' John Joe said . . . and I was filled with a great joy.

'Maybe it's not the end after all,' I said. 'Maybe, it's only the beginning.'

Rose was looking at me with her eyes as astonished as if she had seen a vision, but she might know that there was a good chance that it was the whiskey that had been talking, not I.

'It's something the old mistress said to you on her death-bed. Did you know, Sister Mark, that Constance Peppard had the gift of looking down the years?'

Rose crossed herself and inside in myself I fully recognized that I was almost certainly a false beacon of hope that would lead them more on to the rocks, than they already were.

'She said that a person would come pushing through the thicket of the years. She saw it all that day, and she standing on the threshold of heaven. She saw you building the whole place back to what it's meant to be. I was kneeling in the corner. I saw the way you comforted her, as if you were your mother all over again.'

'It's worth a try,' I said. 'But now I think it's time we all went to bed. It's been a long day. Likely there's worse to come. Let's make a brave start tomorrow morning.'

The next day, I went out and found a camp of tinkers at the avenue gates . . . misjudged them as honest and allowed them to bring their caravans in on the land. They could camp there and help put up another barn from the timber and the bracken. They could round up the goats and see them productive. They could shoot what game there was to shoot and Rose would give them milk and eggs.

I got full-time work in the town to nurse a grocer, who had pneumonia. I was day nurse and night nurse too, so I did not see the castle for two weeks. The grocer better, I returned to Cormac's Castle and found no tinkers, no goats, six missing trees, a great many missing hens and no eggs.

I knew that I had been taken for a mug. At least I had my earnings in my pocket and after I had seen what had happened, I decided to climb the roof again and check that the tiles were still there. I put the ladder against the side of the house and was comforted to see John Joe's work and mine still held fast, and that the tinkers had overlooked the lead. It was wonderful to stand behind the battlements and see the vastness of the Atlantic stretched out in front of me. The ships were child's toys, far out to sea and the sun was shining.

Down in the garden, there were herbs growing and the kitchen was so warm that drowsiness overtook me. I made an 'omelette aux fine herbes' for the grocer's wife had given me a parcel out of the shop, as a parting present. I came to, an hour later asleep on the kitchen table with my head on my arms.

'The day-old cockerels is doing finc,' John Joe said. 'Don't mind them old tinkers. That might have happened to anyone, that wasn't used to their goings on. I've made a start on the second barn myself.'

I looked at him, still more than half asleep.

'We've got a clutch of goose eggs and a clucking hen, Miss Mark. There's a fine orchard of grass out there. It would bring up a hundred goslings . . . '

But always I remembered the little foxes.

Yet we crept by. My grandfather was drinking again, but he had fallen into a mental torpor. Most of the days, he spent sitting by the grave and his mind was blurring. He appeared at the house, as soon as darkness fell and maybe it was wine and maybe it was whiskey. We did our best to make him slow down, but I knew the battle it would have been, even with the whole might of the hospital Psychiatric Unit behind me. Here the fight was lost, as soon as it was joined.

The clucking hen and her brood of goslings cheered us on towards victory. I spent some of my money on bonhams to fatten into pigs for market . . . It was a busy day on the farm now, with the milking to do and the butter, and potatoes to boil up in a copper for the pigs. It was time to try to refurbish the house and this we did by buying tins of paint and wallpaper and a great deal of whitewash.

Looking back now, I can see myself clad in blue dungarees, liberally splashed with white, glad that the ceiling of the kitchen was done and I had only the walls to do. Rose was below at the table, engaged in remaking some curtains from upstairs, on a very old treadle Singer, into cheerful patchwork curtains, that transformed the huge 'acreage' we used as a common room, for living and eating and working. The doctor had promised to send for me the moment he wanted nursing for another private patient. As it was, cases went into the County Hospital, if they needed expert care, past home nursing, by the family.

The grocer had it that it was cheaper than a funeral if a man employed his own private nurse . . . and I knew that he was grateful to me. I thought of him at the counter and how taken he had been with the old red-lined navy cloak and the pristine aprons and that cap with the bow under the chin. I knew I would get more cases . . . hoped I would and knew myself wicked to have such appalling thoughts.

'Please let Mr. Bun, the baker, fall sick! *Mea culpa!* Not terribly sick . . . '

All the time, I corresponded with 'the Proff' and he was very concerned about me, replied to me and did me much harm in telling me the latest news of the department and how they missed me. Still, he was quite certain, I was doing the right thing and the way was open for me to come back again at the top level, if and when I was ready. Just for now, what I was doing was not in any way my duty, but because I was, who I was, I must make it my duty. He confided in me that he found the same sort of situation happened to him and he had never managed to escape, doing what he felt should be done. In the next life, he was determined that he would care for nobody but himself and he advised me to put my name down for the same sort of future existence . . .

I smiled and kept his letter in the breast pocket of my dungarees and so moved on to the great hall, where John Joe had scrubbed the floor to white stone blocks. Rose had velvet curtains waiting to go up again on mahogany poles and the curtains on big wooden rings . . . and I defied the ceiling to break my spirit. It was just a matter of turning off the present and making myself sit in on a ward round and there I was, with the armful of records in my hand . . . and the tea on its way on a trolley and I must speak to the ancillary about her dirty fingernails and the fact that she must not leave the spoon in the cup to show it had sugar in it . . . and the smell of the hospital all about me and the mad traffic that medicine had become . . . and the hint of ozone in X-ray, and the leaded clothing against the killer, that came out of machines . . . and how it was time to go into isolation with the patient for treatment and there was Walt Disney painted on the walls and piped music, in rock and roll. At the last moment, I must leave a lonely person and throw the switch and see the gantries had brought the machine over . . . look through the window, that was a goldfish tank . . . and smile . . . smile . . . smile . . . not think that it was only a chance, if it worked, but we counted it a success after five years of living on . . . and sometimes, it did work.

Cormac was not finding credit at the local shops. He took to dishonourable searching for money, that was lying about the castle, and he would take it, even from the most humble of his faithful retainers and my heart was sore for him. We knew the full shame of alcohol addiction. We knew that we had to keep our money well hid.

I got another nursing job and got out the spick and span uniform again and was very happy for a month, away from the castle and seeing a local farmer learn to walk again, after a Charnley on his hip in Dublin, see him looking at me and saying 'But there's no pain any more, there's no pain and I'll be able to drive the jeep round my acres . . . '

So we crept up and up and I thought we were going to do it, even with Cormac a sheet anchor on our stern. All we had to do was to work every hour God sent and the ends met . . . just. So the days dragged into weeks, and weeks into months and a year was gone. Some of the rooms were redecorated and habitable. There was money to meet the fodder bills. The outside of the house was started and the glass windows replaced. All our stock had shelter and food and there were potatoes in clamps against the next year. Once Regan came to visit us and Goneril with her, to spy out the land. I had just got back off a case and entertained them in the drawing-room and rode them off, with great pleasure, proud in uniform and with great authority.

I pondered if it would be worth my while to ask them if they would like Indian or China tea, but as I had no China, I forebode the pleasure it would have given me to look at their faces . . . and pride went before a fall. It always does. Why will I never learn it?

Our cows were at full yield. We had just sold the pigs at profit and we had filled the barn with a new issue of piglets. We had hens clucking and eggs hatching. We had geese grazing ready for Michaelmas. We had as much butter and milk and eggs as we could manage and customers eager for them. In the town, our butter was famous. We could sell as much as we could make . . . We were happy, happy, happy and Lear was becoming resigned to the death of my grandmother.

We were going to make it. It was almost certain that we had turned defeat into victory. The house was presentable and the farm was thriving. Fanny, the Jenny donkey, was the transport to the town with the produce and there was no pride about me, that I was ashamed to sit in the market and sell butter and eggs and cream . . . and maybe give away some medical advice on the side, for I was building a reputation with no foundation, that I was better than any doctor, for the fame, I had beyond in England . . .

Then one night, came a storm, such I had never seen. The county had never seen such a tempest in living memory. Who was I to have been wise enough to insure against such acts of God?

It poured down rain from the heavens and the stream turned into a torrent. The lamp on the wall of the big barn blew over into the straw and then fire was king. It leaped from one building to the next, the spirit of the fire, jumping from one truss of straw to the next and nothing to stop it . . . and on to a shed and another shed and then to the second barn and we had sweated at all that enclosure of buildings. Worse, they were inhabited with living creatures, the piglets, the geese and the chickens. Fire took the whole lot of them and the sheds and the barns too and laid the land waste. There was nothing left for all our work. The flames beat us back. I got the Jenny donkey out alive and that was the sum total of my efforts. The fire licked the side of the house. It caught the end gable and took hold. It ran along the wood work and filled the whole house with black smoke and we put it out with buckets of water, flung on the nearest blazing point, we could see.

There was a tempest after it, the like of no tempest that had ever been seen before. It laid the silver birches flat on the ground, but they stood up again, when the ferocity was gone. There was no standing up for the small helpless pigs and the hens and the geese . . . no cows ever to milk any more. My grandfather stood on the top step of Castle

Cormac and a Waterford glass in his hand to smash it down at his feet.

'All right then. May the devil take Cormac's Castle and good luck to him!' he shouted.

We had a smell of roast pork and nothing alive in the barn and paint blistered on the front door of the castle and the glass panels cracked in the side windows.

'There's the end of it,' I said dully and knew that I had been a total failure, but Cormac had his hand on my arm.

'You had it beaten. I weighed heavy against you in the balance, but you had it beaten.'

I turned and looked at him. I was sorry.

'Poor Humpty Dumpty!' he said. 'You did your best to put me together again for Constance's sake . . . and your own mother, Cordelia, but the Lord didn't want Humpty Dumpty put together any more. I've broken a fine glass the same as I'd do always . . . the way I've broken my life . . . and the lives of others. Now I'm on a noble course. I'm away to find another glass to drink damnation to my Creator, for I've destroyed a whole family.'

He looked back at me from the front door and the dawn breaking overhead.

'God cursed me that day I sold your mother's grey mare. He cursed me for what I did to that proud lady my wife. He cursed me for doing a devil's trick . . . to dare to give a thing and take it back again . . . when it was not mine to give away . . . not any more.'

The dawn had come and the storm was over. I was wearing my old nurse's gaberdine coat, when I climbed to the cliffs and stood on the very edge of the south coast of Ireland and looked out over the Atlantic. The gulls were wheeling with cruelty in their yellow beaks, as they came down in a swoop to feather my face. Then they glided out on the thermals, with no effort whatever . . . and I surely knew what effort was?

They had nests in the high cliffs and they feared for their young at the hands of a marauder. At the last moment, when they had seemed certain to strike at my face, they were up and away, for they had nests in the long face of that tremendous cliff and come spring . . . merciful heavens, it was spring again now, they had nests to guard against predators . . . fledglings to feed.

I wondered if I too had had fledglings to feed. If I had, I had made a poor hand at it. Here I was, in my worn gaberdine, any nurse on a holiday over from England, with time on my hands for relaxation. I had my collar up round my neck and the blood-red hood loose round my shoulders. It was high time I was buying myself a new coat, but there was no money left, not for new coats.

I stood on the edge of one of the highest cliffs in the world and looked down thousands of feet at the slug of the sea, that tried to climb up to me. It had no chance of ever reaching me any more that I had any chance of recreating the castle. The waves fell back into the cuckoo spit of the sea, yet they turned to climb again and I knew how they felt. God have mercy! I knew how they felt.

Here was a cruel sea, a wrecking sea. A full-crewed ship might be lost here and no trace ever found, but a few flung timbers, that drifted in, on the flow of the tide. They said you could hear the cries, an odd time, of drowned sailors still haunting the night. There was no softness here, no mercy, only the hardness, that was nature. Here was no loving tender care, that I had been groomed to achieve, half my life.

The wind was freshening again and the blackness would come down again before the night. Perhaps I stayed up there all the day . . . and time had run away, but it looked as if night had come again and last night had been a thing of terror . . . such terror, that was unbearable . . . and all the small creatures dying, crying for help, when we could not help them.

I had the uniform of a high qualified sister of medicine under the gaberdine coat, but it had in no way helped me to save life. They were all dead, all the small creatures I had loved . . . all gone and the smell of burnt feathers and roast pork, and Charles Lamb could never have loved the small trusting friendly piglets. It was going to rain again and the wind was rising, but there was no more it could do. I had no fine clothes to spoil. There was a fob watch, on my left shoulder under my coat. I looked at the time, but could make nothing of it. How could I have stayed up here all day on the edge of a cliff, when my duty was at the farm? God only knew what they were making of the devastation! I should be there, but I was afraid to turn my face down the hill and go back to it. I was like a burnt child that dreads the fire. There was a badge on my other shoulder. You could read that I was Sister Mark and it meant nothing to me in this lonely place. 'Sister Mark?' Who was 'Sister Mark?' Why did they want her back in England?

A great gull came screaming out of the sky and feathered against my cheek and made me step back quickly and there was blood on my face. Then the heavens were opening again and we were to have another flood. The sky was as black as Good Friday and the veil of the temple was rent in twain from the top to the bottom and lightning that jig-jagged into my eyes.

There was a mist, that crept up from the sea. If I stepped off the cliff now, I might step into cotton wool and never know the pain, that was death . . . but well I knew the pain that was death. Out at sea, the white horses of Mannanan McLir rode the waves and I might catch a white horse and ride it to Tir Nan Oge. I had but to shift one foot six inches forwards . . . and I would say farewell to all the striving after something, I had never even recognized.

I thrust my hands deep into my pockets and knew there was no escape, not easy escape like that. The rain was wetting my hair, but it could make it no darker nor me any wetter and what did it matter in the universe . . . I was only an unfulfilled nurse, who had taken a wrong turn in life and had lost herself and was not to be found. Not in a hundred years, could I find the thicket that lay round Cormac's Castle and fight my way through it.

The thunder had started to crash again. There was going to be another night of storm, but the damage was done. I had chosen to carve my own way in life and all that was left was the sea, that crept up from the breakers . . . no sweetness and light, no loving tender care . . . nothing but a trap, that I had been caught up in and there was no walking away from it even now. I had promised, but had I meant it at the time? Could I walk away now and I knew the answer before I asked it. There was no walking away . . . never . . . never . . . never . . .

I turned my back on the land and looked up at the low clouds and fired my wrath against God Himself.

'Are you really up there, God?'

My voice wasted on the wind.

'Is it all a great confidence trick? Are we puppets on Your string? Is death a sleep and a forgetting? I don't care if that's the way of it. You don't let nurses have all that much sleep, do You and now I know I'm being impertinent, when I should be on my knees to You. I've been on my knees so many times, and I've learnt the way You run the world. I've seen You gather up the little children, because you love them. I've seen the ones You've let live. Always, always or almost always, You pick the best. Do You never think of empty hearts and broken lives? Is there any heavenly ruling to it all? Is it just a flick of the fingers . . . a cast of the dice . . . a great glorious game played out for eternity?'

There was a flashing of lightning that was

almost continuous now. I turned round and went to the edge of the cliff and was blinded by it and I spat into His face, for the anger, that was still in me.

'You take the happy ones. You leave behind the misshapen ones. You take a man from his wife . . . never think he won't see his children grow up. They'll miss him and he'll miss them. You let teen-aged tramps discard their babies down the sluices . . . and you leave women, who might be loving caring mothers, childless . . . bitter . . . No more babies and a home without happiness . . . I've seen it. I know. You had only to stretch out a hand and a baby would live . . . take one breath and then another and the pinkness of life coming in the white face.'

I went a little way down the hill and the sun came out from behind the thunderheads, when it was like to shine no more. The small wild orchids were a carpet for my feet, as if He meant to make an apology to me, but there was no thought in my head that anybody 'Up there' might hold me in any regard whatever. I sat down on a grassy hillock and my head in my hands and my hair dripped down my back. I was finished with the old way of life . . . the path of achievement. I had left it too far behind me. I had stretched my capability of work to the limit and the thread had snapped. I had done good work and it had got me nowhere. I had been thrown into a dustbin with slippery sides, from whence I could never escape. Even now, I could never leave them, never get back my shining world of science. I had chosen the House of Jackdaws and there I must stay and that day I whispered that there was no future to it and I knew that for once, the Devil spoke true words.

The tiles would soon be dropping like autumn leaves again, and again there would be no tea in the caddy and Mrs. Bun, the baker's wife, might never get ill. The devil whispered to me to go back and pack my bags that very night . . . to clear off, before the Jackdaws took everything I possessed, but I possessed nothing, only a few degrees on parchment.

'I promise you that you've tried,' said the Devil in my ear. 'Nobody will ever be able to say, you've not tried.'

I got to my feet and thought that that was true at any rate. It had just been bad luck, but was there any power on earth that could haul the House of Jackdaws to its feet again, not after this last tremendous defeat? I might grow mushrooms on the floors, but who would buy mushrooms, when they'd soon be growing for the picking in the fields?

I wondered if maybe I was a jackdaw myself. Maybe I was meant to tumble through the skies and bring jocularity to others. If I were a jackdaw, I would find a vertical cavity. I knew the way, they went on. First there was the chimney to find and then, more important, the lodging stick. You found one twig after the other and you dropped it down the vertical funnel. You tumbled into the seriousness of the rooks, returning from their labours in the fields after a hard day's work. Always you dropped twigs down chimneys, till you found the starting stick that lodged, and then you could build. You had a basis for a nest and I had thought I had had a basis, but it had burnt up, as a jackdaw's heap of twigs will burn up in a grate . . . all the effort destroyed. Nothing was left now but a cold deserted hearth and a pile of dry grey ash . . . and that was my present state precisely put. I might have to build another day, but I could not see myself doing it. I had been a jackdaw, when I had a chance to make something out of my life.

I turned at the foot of the rise and ran my hand through my soaking hair. The wind had veered south and you could hear the murmuring of the sea.

'Why don't you watch what goes on down here, God?' I whispered. 'Why don't You let plans be successful an odd time? You can't say I didn't try. All my life I've tried.'

Then I shrank down inside myself, knew the sin of pride and the guilt of it, crossed myself against harm and smiled as I remembered a night in the Convent School, when the Superior had cautioned me against pride. The Superior had painted God in a white nightshirt, as a very elderly stern old man, but I knew He was no such thing. He would never be a benevolent man. He'd be sharp and big business, as like as not. He would sit at a Chippendale desk, genuine, and a chair to match it. He might regard me over horn-rimmed glasses, or maybe the more modish topless spectacles, to strike fear into my chest.

'Maybe, I'll give you some backing, Sister Mark,' He'd say. 'You do realize that you have to produce collateral. I don't bet on losers. Maybe, I used to, but I've given it up recently. After all a person has to help themselves . . . '

His suiting would be clerical grey in a Savile Row cut and his tie, public school of the highest echelon . . . Eton or Harrow or Winchester.

'You've come down badly this time, but you might think of a mortgage, but then, there's the interest percentage. Have you thought about percentage? Things aren't easy on the market. I'll send an agent to discuss what may be done, but I'm getting very weary of being taken for granted. A prayer here and a prayer there, and the whole thing signed and sealed and delivered. We'll see. We'll see what transpires, but frankly . . . there's more to it than that.'

I laughed and saw the evening star clear above my head and I stretched out my arms to it. The Superior had been right about my pride but she had added imagination too. It mattered nothing. I knew it was a fine thing that I could ever laugh again, when I looked back down the last year.

It was going to be a clear night and I was going back to the House of Jackdaws and my black mood was gone.

There was a rumble of thunder again and it chased me down into the valley.

'Why don't you do something about it yourself?' God had asked me, or had He . . . and that was that was that . . .

3

Interval in the life of a stranger

It was somewhere in the south of Ireland, near enough to the harbour at Cove, and it was government property. It was surrounded by a high fence and it was patrolled. There were notices of *KEEP OUT* every few hundred yards. In a room on the first floor, there was a young man, with the air of having authority about him. He stood at the window looking at the sky, thinking that the storm of last night was not finished yet. He hoped that it would not come back to the coast. It might make the *operation self destruct* that bit more difficult, though the game seemed easy enough.

There was a knock at the door and a man came in, somebody he knew, a well-set up chap, six feet tall, but with a slight stoop to his shoulders . . . fifty plus, good Scots tweed suit, chestnut brogues . . . Sherlock Holmes hat, thrown down on the bed now . . . greying hair and his voice matching the tweed of the suit.

'Good day to you, laddie. You'll be wearied

wi' the waiting but we've found a suitable volunteer at last . . . same blood group, matched in every detail. I've come to collect your contribution to the affair . . . '

They wasted no time in the check over of the zip-up bag . . . one uniform, black naval broadcloth . . . suitable insignia, cap with gold braid, black socks, shoes, white handkerchief, black tie, wallet with driving licence, etc, etc, etc. There were twenty three pounds in Irish money and some loose silver, an A.A. membership card, two theatre seats to a show in Cork City. The clothes were newish, but worn and they were marked with the owner's tabs. There was an identity disc, with rank and number . . .

'We'll get started then. Take care. You're a good lad. We'll miss you . . . '

It was near evening, when the young man put on the G.I. uniform, thinking that here was the kit of another country. The crêpe-soled shoes certainly had it over British army boots . . . 'Boots, boots, boots, boots, marching up and down again', but that was another war and this was no war at all, unless . . .

He looked at his reflection in the mirror and read the name tape back to front . . . MICHAEL GRANT. That individual would be any dead soldier. They would have made sure of it, a man with no family and no connections, no one to come looking for him . . . a man without importance, but with the right vital statistics and the right blood group. Michael Grant had no further part to play in the story, but he himself must make sure of detail. Just for now, there must be no doubt that he was Michael Grant. The night was coming down quickly and the storm muttered on the horizon. It was going to be a repeat performance of last night, but now it was time to go.

Presently, he walked out on the tarmac and his driver had the car ready, a car that would turn any man's head to look at it . . . black Mercedes, as shining as a beetle's back, high-powered . . . sleek long bonnet . . . staff car number one, used by Top Brass only, the car he always used himself. They thought the mission important enough to sacrifice staff car number one. It was a pity and he would be sorry to see her go. He looked up at the sky. It was a pitch black night and the cloud low. All the better for what had to be done . . .

The driver had opened the door and he bent his head to get in behind the familiar wheel. The passenger was already in place, safety belt secure. He fastened his own belt and closed the door.

'Good luck, sir. You'll have a quiet companion.'

He put his hand across to rest on the passenger's hand and thought it as cold as any stone . . . remembered Shakespeare and Falstaff . . . 'as cold as any stone'. Trust Shakespeare to get the right sound to his words . . .

The engine started as it always did. It was quite difficult to know it was running, for there was a gust of wind from the south, that set the clouds racing. Then the outer gates swung open and they were through and away up the road, with a smart salute to see them on their way. There was no need to consult maps. There had been a dummy run. There was no need to look at the lighted compass on the dash. He knew the way like the palm of his hand. There were Chesterfield cigarettes in the breast pocket of his jacket and he put one between his lips, but did not offer one to his colleague, just pressed the automatic lighter and waited till it popped out again. The tip of the cigarette glowed as he pulled at it and he glanced at his companion, noted the gold braid on the down-bent cap, the scrambled egg at the cuffs.

'I don't know where or when you left the world before, my friend,' he said. 'Tonight, when the time comes, you'll know nothing about it.'

A car came at them out of the night and they were caught for a moment in its head-lights. It was a strange feeling to see the man, who sat by his side, as like himself as an identical twin. He must drive carefully. An accident would mean disaster and the roads were devilish twisty and narrow . . . a small cottage to starboard and another to port and then nothing for ten minutes. The cottage doors were shut against the threat of another storm like the one last night. It had blown trees down all over the country and it seemed set on appearing for a repeat show of strength tonight, but there was no time for delay. It was near enough to midnight, when he turned on to the dirt road that led up and up again, out towards the rim of the Atlantic . . . to the top of one of the highest cliffs on the south coast, Here was the big rock they had used as a marker, to keep him on his bearings. Now soon, he must pick the very edge of the cliff. It had started to rain and the wind was at half gale, driving the drops horizontally against the screen. A shaft of lightning floodlit the sky and soon after his heads picked up the cliff edge and there was nothing to wait for now. He slowed down and crept up the very edge and got out of the car, stood beside it, with the thunder rolling all about him. He had only to step aside and slam the door, let the car run on down the slope. This was it. The car would run slowly the last few feet. He must take a pace or two alongside . . . then slam the door at the last second. He did not foresee one thing . . . not that the lightning would strike into his eyes at the very last moment of time and the thunder crash down on his head. He was blinded, dazed, and the door was open beside him. He delayed just a twentieth of a second too long. The door gathered him and moved on. The car teetered at the edge and swung over slowly, tilted front wheels down, then made a slithering glissade and a further tilt and it was gone, grating against the sharp edge and bumping from one rock to another. It fell like a shot gannet. It turned over and over, before it reached the sea. There was nobody to see the white splash, as it hit the water and the rocks . . . a child's toy thrown into a deep rocky ocean, a white upsurge for a few moments, some bubbles that rose for a while . . . and lightning again and thunder right overhead, but there was nobody on the cliff to take note of it. There was nobody to see or be seen . . . nobody to say an act of contrition. Nobody to say 'God have mercy on their souls' Who could survive such a fall? The driver had gone to the green grave, and there had been the man who sat in the passenger seat. It had not been planned to happen that way. Just one vicious slash of lightning had cancelled out OPERATION SELF DESTRUCT.

Perhaps there was a chance it might still work in some sort of miraculous way, but miracles did not happen. It had altered the course of the life of one very important man. That much was certain. It was the hand of God had done it. There was no other possible explanation, nor ever would be . . . maybe it had been planned to come about, the way it did. There is nobody to say . . . only the cliff top was quite empty.

4

Somebody sent me he said

I had been angry at God and now I was afraid. One day soon, I must pack and get out of this fortress besieged, in full retreat from adversity, knowing myself a coward. I tried to make excuses, by saying that Cormac had brought every last bit of misfortune on himself. It had all started when he had decided to think he could carve out destinies for his daughters. He had been full of power, a wealthy man, an autocrat . . . addicted to praise. He had accepted the fulsome flattery and rebuffed the candid answer. In that one gesture, he had thrown his happiness away, certainly his wife's, my grandmother's . . . almost surely my mother's well-being, Cordelia, Mark One.

He had been left with this great gaunt castle and some of the lands, that ran with it, but there was no capital to spare. The farms had been taken over and absorbed and his two elder girls were well off with their dowries and with my mother's lost farm of Innish Bawn split between them. He had told

Goneril and Regan that he would expect backing in his old age . . . had been foolish enough to think that their word was their bond.

My mother, Cordelia, had been turned out just for petty spite . . . she had received Lyre na Greana, which had belonged to her mother. She had tried to make a living on a peasant's farm and the gorse had bloomed bravely, but maybe not for her. The gorse bloomed for my father, right enough, I thought bitterly. He was never done thinking he was in love with one girl or another. Mother and I had clung to each other. After I was born, maybe life was more possible. I know I fell short of what I should have done for her. Even now, I think, uneasily I might have been all she had out of that disastrous marriage . . . I imagine that she died, loving me and forgiving me, for how could I have had the sense to know what went on? I knew my grandfather, vain and proud, with an ear always lifted for praise. I knew that he drank too much. Even when I was very small, I knew that. I was not wise enough then to wonder, if he took it to destroy the pangs of his conscience. Maybe it was analagous to the Brompton mixture for terminal cases, that I was to be very familiar with. There was this false euphoria, but in the days of my childhood, I had never heard of 'euphoria', only knew that 'Lear' was always short of money for the castle. Two aunts had conveniently forgotten the golden promises. The amber, mellow Irish whiskey with the splash of soda and my grandfather could be floated off on a false sea of happiness and content, with deep arm-chairs and his peers about him in the fading grandeur, that was on the way out . . . and his conscience running back and back and back, against the pseudo joy in his heart. One toast after another, a talk about the old days and the future was rosy. Yet maybe he never forgot that he had done my mother a fearful wrong. He had done the devil's trick . . . given a thing . . . taken it back again. He had broken my mother's heart because he did just that . . . sold the little white mare out into anonymity, so that she could never be found again . . . never, never, never. God only knew what had become of her, so that my mother had never told even me . . . had just kept the thought of Bawn in her heart, where it pricked her for the rest of her life, with the dreadful no-knowledge of what had become of a loving beautiful creature, that walked in grace.

It has happened before. It can happen again. Alcoholics Anonymous put a finger into the breach to stop the flood and they do good work. Only never again, must alcohol pass an addict's lips, for as sure as it does, down will come baby, cradle and all . . .

The second night of the storm, we were entertaining the hunt club and I saw that the battle was not even joined. The devils were in the house in every amber glass of whiskey . . . in every toast . . . in every offer of sorrow and condolence in trouble. The Waterford tumblers were out and the bubbles winking at the brim of champagne and not enough money in the house to buy tea. Lear was presiding, the centre of attraction because of his bereavement. Cormac had taken it into his mind to breed a pedigree herd. Regan would give him a start with a few Jersey cows. In three years, he would be winning every cup in the Dublin Show from his own daughter. He was past reasoning it out that his barns were in ruins and his stock, such as it was all burnt. You could still smell the burning, it was such a short while ago. The fodder was gone, as if it had never been . . . corn, hay, sugar beet, sanfoin . . . chicken meal, potatoes . . . roasted in the clamps . . . the last apples cooked on the trees.

'Good luck to the Castle Cormac herd of Jersey cattle!'

Regan did not want to know. Regan had no part in any future plans. It seemed quite likely that they wanted no communication with us. The telephone at Lismore Farm was never answered.

I sat in my one good velvet dress and played hostess at the head of the dining-table at Castle Cormac and I watched the money run down the guests' throats, that we could never pay. I knew despair, but I knew rage too. Maybe I managed to conceal the fact. After the port had gone round and round again, I went upstairs and packed my bags. I had no pity left and no patience, only for Rose, who crept along to my bedroom after a while. I was standing by the bed, looking down at the perfection of my starched uniforms packed carefully in a case . . . a bitter taste in my mouth. Already, I had written a telegram form to 'the Proff', but as yet, it lay on my dressing-table. In two-three days, I would be on my way back and there was no force in the world could hold me in Castle Cormac . . . and still the soft voice said 'Don't walk away'. I looked at my reflection in the mirror, the green velvet dress, the green slippers, my hair down one shoulder in a twisting ringlet. Here was no starched nurse then, no workaday dairymaid, every inch of me the granddaughter of Cormac's Castle, playing hostess to his friends. I had my fare home to England and no more, just that much left in my purse. The uniforms were all ready to put on. I had tried and I had failed. There was no redemption in this grey smouldering fortress. They were downstairs, drinking the very soul of it. It was time Cormac went for treatment in a unit, but I cared no longer. For all I cared, let him go searching the earth like the Wandering Jew, till he found her white mare, that he had sold over Cordelia's head. I had had enough. God knows I had had enough. Rose stood and trembled at my side and said that she did not blame me, but that they would all be destroyed without me. I walked past her and down the stairs and out to the veranda and tried to close my ears to 'Do ye ken John Peel' from the dining-room. John Joe was in the shadow below the rail and he came to look up at me, his face sad.

'You done your best, Sister Mark. God Himself knows. Nobody could have done more. You put back the heart into us and we'd have died gladly to work at your side, there's no sin to you, if you get out of here on the first train. God sent that fire to destroy us and there's no fighting God. We might think to start off yet again, but there the devil that lives in Himself. The doctor says he'll die. It's in my heart tonight to say that the sooner he does it the better it will be . . . '

He had his cap in his hand and he was awkward with me.

'I'll look after the place as best as I can and I'll see to the Jenny donkey, but she'll be lonely after yourself.'

I felt the small doubts infiltrating my soul, and he tried to lay them to rest.

'Nobody will put blame on you to go. It's your last chance at it this minute.'

I turned on him like a virago.

'Of course, they'll blame me. Do you not think I remember what I promised my grandmother . . . that I'd not go. What do you think I'm doing this minute, but going back on a promise made in the last moment of her life?'

The guests were making a night of it and they had come out on the front steps to try to find their cars, the glasses still in their hands and left down anyhow, anywhere, for anybody to clear up after them.

Then they were all gone and John Joe had held my arm to stop me running after them like a mad dog, for the rage in me. We stood side by side on the veranda and listened to Rose talking to the master within the house. Then the light clicked off and there was silence.

I felt Constance Peppard's spirit beside me, as real as if she stood there.

'Just a day or two longer, Mark. Time is slow in eternity. Don't run yet. It's no time for running, just when it's going to start at last . . . have you thought maybe it's only the beginning . . . not the end of it all?'

I spun round to John Joe, but he had heard nothing and there was a man coming walking up the drive to us to stand wearily at the bottom of the veranda steps. The moon had come out from behind the clouds and the light shone his hair. There was rain that ran down his face and he wore a uniform sodden with wet, dark instead of olive drab. The lightning was so brilliant that it illuminated his name tab for me and I was used to such things in the hospital . . .

MICHAEL GRANT

There was a swathe of black hair stuck to his forehead and his eyes bewildered.

I thought he was in a state of shock, but he spoke in a calm enough voice, apologized that he was disturbing the house at a very late hour. He weaved a little on his feet and I thought that he was just another drunken man and John Joe was of the same mind. He was a G.I. Joe, dishevelled after some party on rye whiskey. The light shone off his black hair and the rain ran down his face and soaked his green tunic. He was slurring his words, weaving like a shadow boxer.

'I think I had an accident, ma'am. I might have hit my head. I can't remember. There's a fool thing . . . can't even recall who I am. You're the first person I've met . . . or perhaps you are . . . the first house I've seen, except for cottages with lit eyes and that was a while back.'

I thought he looked ill, rather than drunk.

'Nobody must know,' he whispered to me. 'But nothing will stay in my head . . . '

He saw that I looked down at his name tab in the next flash of lightning and his hand slapped up across to hide it from me, clutching the rail of the balustrade with one hand and covering '*Michael Grant*' with the other.

'It's all right, Michael Grant,' I said. 'It can't be much of a crime to be Michael Grant, but are you ill?'

'I don't seem to have any hurt. Only my head aches a bit. I'd like to lie down but they say one must keep walking . . . sleepy or cold . . . walking, walking, walking, on and on and on, or you die. But then, I was supposed to die, wasn't I? I've forgotten it all.'

My hand was at his pulse and mentally I registered *too slow*. There was a cut at his temple, that bled down his face. He was any soldier arriving in casualty after a drunken night, but there was no reek of alcohol from him . . .

He went slowly down on his knees and pitched forwards onto his face and John Joe reappeared out of the dusk with a horse blanket.

'He's dead drunk, Sister Mark, leave him to me. I'm used to it by now.'

I had discovered the torn fingernails and the scraped chest, that had bloodied his shirt. He was coming to his senses again.

'Go and fetch the doctor, John Joe. Get him here as quickly as you can.'

The stranger was clinging to my hands to stop me . . . flinching at the pain from torn nails.

'It's very important. Please let me go. Don't say you've seen me. If you could let me hide here. It's terribly important, yet I don't want you snarled up in it. I can't remember why, but it's top priority. I mustn't be found . . . not ever. Oh, God! Why can't I remember? It's a dream, I dreamt, but it was real and there was no sense in it. If I'm found now, it will blow the whole thing apart. Rather than be found, I must die. It would have been for nothing . . . '

John Joe had lost patience with both of us and was wrapping the man in the horse blanket, asking me if I did not recognize when a chap had drink taken.

130

'God save us, Sister! This is man's work. Keep out of it. I'll shove his clothes by the stove in the kitchen and they'll dry out. He'll dry out himself by then. He can be on his way. He'll sleep it off on a lock of straw and be no better of it, come the morning. He's from the Yankee camp across the mountain. I'll turn him in that direction come daylight. I'll have got shut of him before you're up.'

There was no smell of alcohol. His pulse was slow. He had a head injury and a slow pulse. His finger nails looked as if he had been tortured. There were stranger things being done in Ireland. He was no G.I. not by his voice. He was British Army, probably down from Ulster . . . maybe British Navy from Cove. At a guess, he had crashed his car. It was always the simplest explanation . . . victim of a hit and run perhaps? Who could possibly have tortured a person in the south of Ireland? Yet his finger tips were terribly injured. Maybe he had clawed at something very sharp and rough.

'He's hurt!' I said. 'He's not drunk. He's badly shocked.'

That was a joke to John Joe.

'Ach, no, Miss Mark! The next thing you'll be on about is that he's on the run. This chap's a G.I. Joe. What would he be running from? I ask you that.'

Michael Grant had started to mutter about the lightning. For a moment, I remembered my revolution against heaven on the cliff top. It was quite impossible that this man had been heaven-sent to me, because of my demands . . . my accusations . . . but the thought restored my sense of humour.

'We get Michael Grant upstairs and into bed. We dress his wounds and we keep him under observation, John Joe. If we had any sense, we'd send for a doctor and if he gets any worse, that's what we'll do. Meanwhile, let's get on with it.'

So we got on with it and still, the man muttered about the lightning and John Joe never stopped telling me how little sense I had in my head.

I stood at the head of the bed at last, when we had got him settled comfortably, and by then I had taken off my fine dress in exchange for a towelling shirt and slacks. I was not going to risk messing up that one fine velvet gown.

The fingers were all bandaged neatly in gauze and the wound on the temple dressed with a sterile adhesive strip. He was wearing blue pyjamas that John Joe had produced from somewhere and now he was not lucid. I stood by the bed and he looked up at me and frowned in puzzlement.

'He calls you Sister Mark and sometimes he calls you Miss Cordelia. You're the gentle one and your sisters are witches. That was the way of it, but I don't know where the nursing sister comes into *King Lear*. I did it at school. I was in love with Cordelia, when I was fourteen years of age, going on for fifteen . . .'

It was high time to get medical advice, but I had only to suggest it, to make him agitated. I knew I should be thinking of neuro-surgery and the coroner might have something to say to me in a day or two. The man was past making his own decisions. If I had been at the New Site, I should have picked up the nearest phone and bleeped the Neurosurgical Registrar. As it was, I was fool enough to trust my very strong intuition that this man was in big trouble and not just because he had a head injury and torn nails. There was a red alarm about the whole case. There was danger all about us, but I did not know from what direction it threatened. There was a civil war tearing Ulster to bits. I concentrated on the important thing of observation and general nursing care and knew that as usual I was being a fool. Always the torn nails worried me and here I was, a fly caught on a sticky paper. If I had been going to report it, I should not have delayed. Now I sat by his side all night and sometimes I held his bandaged hand in mine and now and again, I sponged his face. Always I talked to him calmly and kindly and tried to assure him that he would be fine. I had seen to everything and it was going to be all right. I knew it as the under-statement of all time. The hours passed, till by the light of day, he was clearer in the head . . . able to take some tea and a finger of buttered toast . . . able to fall into a sleep . . . to wake at midday, his brow in a crease at once, wandering again.

'Cordelia married the King of France,' he told John Joe and John Joe was not impressed by that, only muttered to me that he hoped I knew what I was doing and asked me if I had seen the state the gentlemen had left the dining-room in, last night. The master was still in his bed and maybe I'd better have a look at him, while I was about it.

'Maybe you've got two dying men on your hands,' he said, but Michael Grant was telling me that I had a lovely name and that the King of France was a lucky man.

'You married the King of France.'

'You're wandering a little. Don't worry. It will pass in a few hours.'

I went off and saw to Lear, but there was no worry about his hang-over. O'Brien was giving him some restorative, that was spiked with Worcester Sauce, and was well in control of the situation. Back with my neurosurgical case, I bent my head to hear what my patient was saying and heard him clearly.

'I'm not wandering, Cordelia . . . '

His voice was very pleasant.

'So we'll go no more a-roving
So late into the night,
Though the heart be still as loving
And the moon be still as bright . . . '

Here a sigh and a long pause.

'Though the night was made for loving,
And the day returns too soon.
Yet we'll go no more a-roving
By the light of the moon . . . '

'It's well past noon,' I said. 'It will soon be evening again. Try to have some soup. Rose sent it up for you. Then you'll go to sleep again. Tomorrow is another day. It will all come back.'

He drank his soup, turned on his side like a little boy and went to sleep and he slept like a dead man all the night, till sometimes I wondered if he was still alive . . .

Rose had cleaned up the dining-room and the hall. John Joe had swept up all the broken glass. The old man was wandering about the house, very repentant, after two nights in bed.

John Joe and I were very disconsolate, though we said nothing. We had worked hard to build up the nucleus of the farm and had seen it blaze to a ruin before our eyes. If the stranger had not come walking up the drive, I would have been on my way to England by this time. Almost certainly, I would have forgotten my promise not to walk away. This was indeed the House of Jackdaws and for some new reason, I was still here.

My grandfather had arrived downstairs repentantly on the second day, grumbling, groaning, repentant, but I had no sympathy with him any more. The tinkers had made off with our wood and our stock. The fire had burnt the rest. King Lear had had his friends in to dinner and sent us spinning back into the red . . . and the smell of burning still invading the whole place and beasts lying unburied . . . new built barns totally destruct. The farm had been consumed by fire, all of what we had achieved. I remembered painting the door of the house, the door of Castle Cormac in perfect cream. I had shone the brass dolphin knocker. Now the paint was bubbled and black and the knocker was running a stream of green down the door. The weeds had taken encouragement. They had started springing up again between the stones of the steps.

'Isn't the front door ruined with blisters?' John Joe asked me . . .

Dear God. If ever there was a Jackdaw, it was I! I might tumble through the air, dive and twist and spin, but I could never escape. I had found a vertical cavity and I had sought out 'a starting stick'. Maybe it might have been a failure, but that was nothing to a jackdaw. I must start off again. One day, I would find the stick that lodged across this particular funnel. Then I would build a home. It was all a matter of finding a *starting stick* . . . and build on. Just for now my starting sticks had been burnt up on a neglected hearth, but there was always another chance.

Before I left Castle Cormac, there was time for one last try. Maybe the stranger was a starting stick. There must be some reason that he had come in the dark of the night out of nowhere . . . a stranger in a strange uniform and very much in need of my help . . . a young man with gentle manners and a pleasant face, with his wits scrambled. Maybe mine were scrambled too. I yearned to go back to the hospital, but I had not sent the telegram. Besides, I had made that promise. I wanted to be out of this crazy wilderness and home to civilization . . . home to the work, that was full of excitement and importance. I thought back to the modern world, whose walls held ornamental fish tanks, where music played, where people lay and were not afraid, where the gantry moved the giant machine across and down with precision over a pencilled-off area of skin. Radio-therapy was surely the science of the future. It was the big step forwards. I wanted to be there to help, to feel that I was of some use. It must win in the finish, this game, that was played out to the death. There were so many people, whom I knew in the hospital, people who missed me and looked for me.

'Where's Sister Mark then?'

Sister Mark was held prisoner by her conscience in an old ruined fortress. It had a roof that could hold out the rain, but did that really matter? The next storm might take the roof out over the Atlantic in one piece. A good tempest would send the battlements down like the teeth in the Tom and Jerry cartoon . . . and who was I to be amused by that?

I shampooed my hair with fresh water from the rain barrel and tried to think again. Maybe I was ready to start all over . . . to have one more lick at it, but that was folly, yet my hair was like mist, so light and lovely it was. I might walk through the fair and a man would turn to look at me and why should I be thinking such thoughts?

Michael Grant was no ordinary 'head case'. I would stay on for one more day and then another and then another, so that I unpacked my uniform and put it in my cupboard drawers, in case I went into nursing again.

I was ready to start all over. There is no doubt about it. I made over his room into a semblance of a neurosurgical after-care unit. One day, I put on the uniform and it was only to impress him and he was impressed. I wondered if I was crazy, but his wounds healed well. He was able to sustain conversation. After a time, I began to suspect that he did not forget as much as he pretended to forget. He was keeping that fact to himself.

One day, I let him sit in the chair by the window and maybe, it was a week later, or a fortnight and me still staying in the House of Jackdaws and no telegram sent off. I remember that day well. He was wearing an old suit of sky blue pyjamas and he had two pairs of them and I laundered them turn and turn about and that was no work for a top nursing Sister. I recall the camel hair dressing-gown and the old slippers, which had been found by scrounging the house possessions.

His wounds were healing, only for the torn nails. Still I wondered how a man could come by such injuries. The shabby dressing-gown was in no way right for him. He had an aura of dark wine silk dressing-jacket and top notch private home . . . of black quilted satin lapels and monogrammed pocket. I had seen it all. I know it by instinct . . .

Yet he was not clear in his mind yet and it bothered me, that I had not called for expert help. I might have done him an awful injury. We would say a thing and forget it the next moment and return to say it again. Just now, he was sitting by the window, looking down at Cormac picking a bunch of Michaelmas daisies, some late lavender, binding them with the tendrils of a creeping plant that had white trumpet flowers.

'I could do something about the garden for you. I could get those barns to their feet again. I could get this place ship-shape, if only you'd let me help. Give me three-four weeks with John Joe.'

He would say it and return to say it again.

Then he was watching Cormac on his calvary up the trail to the graveyard . . . and presently Cormac down on his knees.

'Why does he do it now, when it's too late?'

he asked me in despair and I shot out at him in return, hoping to stimulate something out of his brain.

'British Navy? That's it, isn't it?'

He shied away from that and would not meet my eye.

'I could get this place ship-shape in four weeks,' he said.

He studied his fingertip gauzes. He would not meet my eye.

'Sometimes, it gets clear and the next moment, it's gone. I'm not sure . . . not really sure. I know I dreamt a dreary dream. I'm dead. I told you. Didn't I? It makes nonsense, the way a dream makes. I have to be dead. That I remember, nothing else very clearly. I mustn't surface . . . or it will all be destroyed and it's very important indeed. I could not begin to tell you, how very important it is . . .'

Then he was lost again, watching Cormac up at the burying plot, his brow frowning and himself indeed lost again.

'I told you, didn't I? I must be dead?'

My grandfather was kneeling by Constance Peppard's grave.

Again came the pleasant voice.

'He's praying that you won't go away . . . that you'll stay on in Cormac's Castle, till you get it all straightened out. I find the same prayer on my lips. I don't know why . . . '

Of course, he would have had my story from John Joe and all the rest of them. There was not one person in the household, that could keep a shut mouth. Rose was the worst of them all for prying into my secret affairs and she had taken to creeping up the stairs with an egg beaten in milk and a dash of sherry in it. Perhaps Michael Grant was skilled in the art of espionage. My skin crawled at the thought.

'You say you dreamt a dreary dream, I lived one here, Michael. You have no idea what a mess I made of it from start to finish . . . I don't even know why I came home.'

'I know what it is to make a mess of things,' he sighed, 'Very important priority things . . . '

'Tell me,' I invited, but still he held out on me and threw dust in my eyes, as if he had not learned that he could trust me, even now.

'It all runs away out of my head. It's a devilish thing,' he said, and I put him back to bed before his time, in anger against him and knew myself very petty and spiteful. I was punishing a small boy, who lay there and smiled at me and refused to be punished. All I could think of was that it was a sin for a man to have such long eyelashes and such dark blue eyes. When he was asleep, I stood over by the window and tried to make an inventory of endeavour. I had nursed an old lady through the last fight of all. I had had a shot at farming and house-building and barn and shed-building and tiling and concreting, and painting. I had collected eggs. I had got up at break of day to milk. On the side, I had taken nursing jobs . . . a common or garden registry nurse. There was nothing any more, not after the holocaust, that had swept the farm and burnt up living animals, concentrating them to a smell of burnt flesh and feathers. I would hear their dying till the day I died myself . . . and nothing I could do. The place had been laid waste. It was barren indeed now and there was no piping water into the desert. There was nothing any more. Oh God! The screaming of the little pigs, that used to press their noses against my legs . . .

So what to do? Grow mushrooms on the damp floors of Cormac's Castle? People had only to wait a few months and there would be mushrooms to spare, growing free in the fields . . . and I was so unhappy that death would be a happy thing, because failure was so bitter. It had been important to me. Michael Grant had said something was important. Well, it had been important to me . . . as important as any case I had ev tackled. It was finished. It was done. I put head down on Michael's bed and I cried like a small child, with gasps and hiccoughs and sobs, my shoulders heaving and the tears pouring down my face. I knelt by his bed and he slept soundly and then his arms were about me.

His voice whispered against my ear.

'You've had a very bad time. They told me all you did . . . all you tried to do. You fought well.'

My words were as jumbled as any heart-broken child's, kept in late at school, afraid never to come home again.

'I can't . . . stay here . . . all my life . . . not for ever. I can't win . . . not here . . . not against Cormac and his castle. The battle was lost a long . . . time ago, lost before it had begun . . . and yet, I promised her.'

He held me against his bandaged chest and his hands patted my back awkwardly. Then he dried my tears with the end of the sheet and I ran away across the room and found a freshly laundered handkerchief, came back and put it on his bedside table and apologized to him for my slipshod nursing.

'There's nothing wrong with your nursing,' he said, and I gave him a watery smile and went to stand looking out through the window again.

'You've broken your heart against this

damned place,' he said. 'If you put all the past history behind you and think of it sanely, you know it wouldn't be impossible to succeed here. You want reinforcements from base,' he said to my back. 'That's all.'

I said nothing and after a little, he went on.

'It's a pity to let an old house like this go ... might as well lose a fine ship. It's a rocky shore below the cliffs out there. It's a long drop to the sea, and it's a wrecking coast.'

How did he know that and who was he, I wondered.

'You had bad luck from start to finish. Even before you came here, there was bad luck. Tear up that telegram, Rose says you've written. We still have John Joe and the O'Briens. We still have timber left over from the operation. There's as much bracken and straw stored at the back of the yard, where the fire didn't reach. I'll rustle up a hen or two, even if I have to go out at night and steal them. There are fish in the sea and I can borrow a boat. The roof's sound. You fixed the outbuildings once. Let's do it again.'

'So you're the reinforcements sent up from base?' I said, still keeping my back to him.

'I can't run in the open yet. Besides, I'd like

to prove something to you.'

He laughed and said that he had a mind 'to go a-roving in the light of the moon' and I spun round and looked at him in surprise.

He was sitting up in bed, his shoulders squared and a look of pride about him, but he was serious again.

'We've seen the old man on his knees by the grave of Miss Constance. There's something terribly important here.'

'Who are you?' I asked him directly.

'My name is Michael. I told you. Maybe I told you it was Grant, but I know now that it's not Grant. For the present I'm Michael . . . '

'But Michael was an archangel.'

'Leave it at that then. I'm Michael, an indifferent archangel.'

It was a joke to him, but I felt a quiver of fear at the nape of my neck. There was all that old superstition, indigenous to the Irish. After all, I had attacked heaven, face to face with dire accusations against the Most High.

'Did somebody send you here?' I asked before I could stop myself.

'Somebody sent me, but not in any way you could think of. It's true that somebody sent me, but whether I made it or not, I really don't know yet. We'll see. There's more to the story. One day I'll explain the way it came about, but just for now, play it my way. Let me stay here and keep out of the way of the world. Let's form a firm company and try to rebuild the fortress. There might be worse ways of passing the long time, till life begins again for you and for me.'

5

The white mare

The day we started for the second time, to rebuild the estate, we stood at the sitting-room window and watched old Cormac returning down the hill from the burial ground one more time. Michael still had sympathy for him, when maybe sympathy was a scarce commodity in the house for 'Himself'. Michael treated 'Lear' with the respect that perhaps we had thrown away.

It seemed to me that day that time had lost counting. There was much we planned to do. There was the material to assemble and we had to provision the house, with scant means.

I am taking as starting day, the day the white mare arrived. As I said, Cormac had been up at the grave and the afternoon was turning into evening. The O'Briens were at household business, scraping some sort of supper together for us in the kitchen. John Joe was hefting what timber there was out to what was already called 'the building site'. It had been time to redress Michael's fingertips and proclaim 'no more dressings from now.

The sheets will heal them' and me hoping that he would not hurt himself with his efforts against the construction of a barn, or his theft of a fowl . . . or maybe with the launching of a fishing boat below on the sea, for there was a way you could come to it, if you went round and round and down a long winding grassy sandy path.

Michael had searched the castle and found treasure, long forgotten. The basement was virtually a dungeon and no longer used, and he it was, who had insisted on opening it up. He had come on a harness room, with tack oiled and preserved, saddles, bridles, dandy brushes, all put into store by a careful groom, but we did not even know his name. Here were hay racks and mangers, feeding troughs, hay forks, all cleaned and polished for the last time and put away . . . as if indeed a wicked spell had been starting to work and the stuff had to last out a hundred years. There was a small cart that fitted the Jenny donkey or maybe a little pony . . . the harness to go with it, the bit shining silver steel . . . oiled against time. There were saddles for horses and every harness imaginable, a governess cart, as good as the day it was made, when the cobwebs were brushed aside . . . the bridle and the harness. The governess cart was in an open garage in the lower storey, but nobody had opened it . . . just sealed it against time . . . and there it was still in the pride of its prime. The way in to it was closed with brambles, but Michael had made short work of them. The leather covered seats might be eaten up by moth, but they were easily replaced, with foam rubber. Foam rubber had been a thing of the future those days. There was enough curtain material hanging about the castle windows to cover a multitude of moth damage.

'I'll put a coat of fresh paint on that governess cart, maybe stripe yellow lines down the spokes with a feather and then do the lot with yacht varnish,' Michael remarked and I knew there was no reality to what he planned. The battle was not joined, but it would be lost, just as the battle before had been lost . . .

We were going to start on the big barn in the morning and we were making plans, when the man arrived down the drive, leading a white horse. We all came out to see what was going on, John Joe from the yard, the O'Briens from the kitchen and Michael and I from the sitting-room. Michael was any man now in khaki slacks and a dark green sweater, that Rose had knitted for him. He had let his beard grow and had trimmed it along his jaw, into Spanish line, that suited him fine . . . and hair on his upper lip too. There was no recognizing him . . .

I saw the local sergeant of police was approaching . . . a guard I knew, getting on towards fifty. Pat Sheehan was his name. He had a white mare on the end of a rope and a rope halter on her, this aged white mare. My mind was split. Michael had no fear of the law, I told myself and in the same breath asked Pat Sheehan what I could do for him, but it was not as easy as that, for this was Ireland. Time was for slaves . . .

I started again . . . said good evening and what a grand day it had been and asked him if the prices had been good at the fair that day . . .

Maybe it was the Spanish beard, that disguised Michael as well, that he no longer feared the Civic Guards, I thought. His hair was longer too and the name tab was out of sight, presumably destroyed.

There would have been beasts in the town today, invading the streets and farmers and jobbers and drovers and tinkers . . . the pubs doing good trade. Rose and her husband were at the top of the front steps. Lear had just reached the bottom of the hill. John Joe was stroking the mare's neck and talking to her softly.

Our conversation was leisurely, as if we

were not all agog to find out what Guard
Sheehan wanted. Rose had run back to the
kitchen for some bits of bread to give the
animal. I held the bread on the flat of my
hand and felt the velvet nostrils snuffle and
the lips take . . . leaned my forehead against
her neck, the white mare.

'Och, yes indeed, it had been a good fair,
too good perhaps, for it had a plague of
tinkers in it and all dead drunk, before long.
Their women were begging the shops and
making trouble too and every man's hand
against them.'

It was not too cold yet. There hadn't been a
good frost and that was why the leaves were
still on the trees. Come a hard day and they'd
drop like the rain, I thought, and here was
Ireland at its best, a soft evening coming on
and the sky pink-red against a good day
tomorrow and silence over the whole world,
or so it seemed . . . and the next day we
would start the work and might God and
Mary bless it!

Now Rose was coming out with a glass
of porter for Guard Sheehan and he said it
was mighty civil of us, for maybe he had
come to ask a favour. Still the porter was
welcome after such a trying day and they
didn't want the tinkers in the cells. It was
best if they cleared off out of the town and

left decent folks alone.

The sergeant had given the rope into my hand and the mare nuzzled against my pocket. She was determined that I give some attention to her. She moved round behind me and butted her nose up against my back and I scratched her withers and asked her what she wanted and her nose dropped in my hand, as if it belonged there . . . soft as velvet.

This place was at the edge of the world. It was an event when a man came walking up the avenue with a white mare.

'Och! of course, ye'll get the barn up and the sheds. Can't you see what God has sent back to ye! Do none of ye recognize her? It's the Colleen Bawn, or so they all had it in the town, the old ones.'

'The Colleen Bawn? The Colleen Bawn?'

She was a fine white mare . . . maybe aged, but still with the pride in her. She was half Arab at a guess and who was I to set myself up as a judge of horseflesh?

O'Brien had not moved from the top step of the front door.

'Jesus, Mary and Joseph! She *is* the Colleen Bawn, but it can't be. It can't be.'

He was in a fugue, a sadness and all the years run away.

Sheehan drained the last of his pint and Rose ran like a small beetle to get him another and still enchantment held us in some kind of spell, that we could never break.

There were cruel galls on the mare's withers. I ran my fingers over them and cursed the men that had so ill-treated a fine animal.

O'Brien was running his hands down the animal's legs like any vet, looking at one ear and then the other to find the clipped notch and triumph in his old man's voice.

'She is the Colleen Bawn. She bears the same mark.'

His face was puzzled and uncertain suddenly.

'But it can't be. It was all long ago. She'll be dead and gone now, unless there's been a miracle to call her up from the dead.'

'There was an old man in the Square today, but he was so drunk, he didn't know what he was saying. He said this was the Colleen Bawn, was Miss Cordelia's, that Cormac had sold away. He said that the Almighty had sent her back again and I had best take her back to the Castle . . . '

There was a pause for thought and then he went on.

'In any case the tinkers had ill-treated a fine beast. The Cruelty Man was after them. I told them to clear off out of the town and I brought the mare here. You'll know what to do with her. The tinkers were for selling her for dog's meat. There's cash that way. I took a chance on what the old man said, drunk and all as he was. If she's the Colleen Bawn, isn't she the mare that brung Cormac Castle down in ruins about Cormac's ears and put the evil eye on the whole place? Ye might be interested in making her welcome here again and the bad luck drawn off ye and ye back in the favour of heaven?'

He took off his cap and mopped his brow, with a light blue handkerchief.

'There was quite a carry on in the town. They were all shouting at me to take the mare back to the castle.'

' 'Ay, take her back to the castle,' they called out, but mind you they were all half cut. 'Let Cormac undo the wrong he done. At least give him a chance to undo it'.'

Then . . . 'I have no place to put her for the night, Sister Mark. Could you take her off my hands? We'll start off again, in the morning, if ye don't want her.'

He went into a confidential talk with me. The mare was starving, but it was only because her teeth wanted filing. By luck the vet had been in town and the sergeant had taken the mare to him. The teeth had been done. Now she would eat well and do well. I could have her as a gift, if only I'd give her house-room.

'She'll crop grass now. She'll live. The tinkers were letting her starve.'

There was an end of the barn still unburnt . . . a loose box, with a cobbled floor. The mare led the way to it and nuzzled into the sweet hay that John Joe brought . . . ate greedily at some mash he provided. Still I did not know the importance of what was happening.

'They said it would be a kindness to have her put down, but I remembered what had gone on at Cormac's Castle.'

She had lowered her head to drink deeply of the fresh water. She had known her way to the loose box, but it was impossible. It was out of joint with time. I had slipped the rope halter off her head and dropped the cross-bar of the loose box and John Joe had bedded her down with clean fresh straw. The night would soon be here. He had found a storm lantern and he set it to swing on the beam. I knew it all fitted in, but I could not see how, only knew a great peace in my soul.

'We can keep her, Sergeant Sheehan? We can really keep her?'

'You're welcome to her, Miss Mark. Nobody else seems to want her. She's yours. Maybe she was once your mother's. There's old ones in the town, that believe that she was.'

A car had come to collect the sergeant and he finished his drink, thanked us and was gone.

'Good luck go with you, Sister Mark. I believe it will be all right now, but I'm not a young man. I believe in the old things and what's right and what's wrong. If I've helped ye, I'm glad.'

He leaned out of the car window.

'They were quite sure in the fair that she was the Colleen Bawn. It's that clip in her ear. A horse can live fifty one years. There was one done it out in Libya. Look in the Guinness Book of Records. It's not impossible that this is the same horse that Cormac took off his daughter . . . sold out from under her . . . destroyed all the luck of the whole estate. It 'tis so, then the luck's come back here tonight. Thanks be to God!'

So maybe that was how the luck came back.

Cormac looked like a dead man. He muttered that of course, we'd take Colleen Bawn . . . we ought never have let her go. No good had come of it. He went away up the steps and the police car was gone in a spray of gravel and the night was upon us and the hurricane lamp glimmered brightly, warmly.

I was remembering the family history that Constance Peppard had told me, the history

157

that my own mother had never mentioned . . . how Lear had taken the mare from my mother and had sold it out of the country and how evil had fallen on the castle, so that the crops went awry and there was ill fortune and no love lost . . . and all was false and unhappy . . . and daughter against father and sister against sister . . . and a whole estate gone to ruin.

Here then was the grey mare, but white now, who had followed Cordelia, my mother, around the stables like a dog and butted her with gentle nose, if she sat on a gate . . . and in the morning, I let her free to explore the bleak stable yard. I sat on the gate and she was behind me and she jumped the generations. I ignored her and presently, her nose was in my back and I found myself pushed off the gate gently into the grass . . . and knew her or thought I knew her as the Colleen Bawn, but there is no proof of it, only in my heart . . . that she came back to us . . . when it was all said and done and over and finished.

She should have been dead a long time, but somehow she had survived. I stroked the soft nose with my hand and whispered into the velvet ear.

'You've found your way home again. Don't ever know that she's gone. I look enough like her for you to think you've found her again and I'll love you and keep you . . . see that nothing evil happens to you ever again. See! Here's an apple in my pocket, the same apple that she'd have had for you . . . and a lump of sugar and a hunk of crusty bread.'

There was joy, as she nuzzled at my hand. I suddenly felt a great faith, that maybe God had been listening to me that day on the cliff. It was the strangest thing the way it happened . . . first the whisper that went round the whole barony.

It blazed like a heath fire and the Irish have no shame of superstition. We confess to believing in the 'little people' and in ghosts and in the fact that it is unlucky to bring May into the house, unlucky to walk across a fairy ring. Who is there to prove it is not?

There was a miracle now coming to pass in the kingdom of Munster, but there was no shame in it, only a great shining happiness, that there was such a person as God, who could look down a time or two, and take pity on the least of things, that was man. It was quite impossible what happened next and it went on happening for as long as the necessity arose.

That first evening, the mare had arrived along the avenue, but she had been seen at the fair. The next day, she had tipped me off the gate and accepted me as her mistress, that was dead and gone. It was big magic.

In the afternoon a small army of farm men arrived along the same avenue, on bicycles and in cars, as if they had nothing better to do, but there was purpose to them. They had heard we wanted help and they wanted to help. There was nothing else much on. It was a slack season. God bless us! They were like nothing as much as the people who won the Middle West of America . . . the settlers who had sought a promised land . . . a land in Wyoming, a land in Oregon, the ones, who had crossed the great plain, the women walking at the side of their men, and the prairie schooners. Here it was all over again, if you half closed your eyes, you could see them walking the earth.

There were women and men and the dress today was denim shirts, denim jeans, and many the men's hair long these modern days, and manners casual too, so very casual, so that nobody's feelings were hurt by charity, for that was what it was.

I knew something about history, but not a lot. I knew that women had worn denim slacks as far back as 1849 and it was all happening again, but they arrived carelessly now. There were no deserts to cross and no wild Indians. There were no wide deep rivers to conquer, but here were the same people, only many years on. They were not class conscious. They came from the humblest cottage and the highest mansion and the introduction was . . . the pass word . . . 'We hear the Colleen Bawn's come back to Cormac's Castle. Maybe it's time we were here.' A little pause then and always the same thing . . .

'God be thanked!'

I could never describe what happened, not in words. The barns and sheds were going up, with uprights and beams of sawn timber, thatched with straw and bracken and it was all there. It was the miracle of the loaves and fishes over again. It just came about and nobody could explain how it happened. Here was split chestnut fencing and areas railed off. Here were straw roofs wired down against the Atlantic gales with great stones and rope. Here were bags and bags of feeding-stuff, kibbled maize, corn, sugar beet pulp, oats, barley . . . hay and straw in great trusses, piled high and coming from out of nowhere.

An old woman in a red shawl would creep in with a setting of eggs and a broody hen and see to establishing it to her satisfaction, in a little pen with a barred front.

'Give her water and a handful of corn and maybe the scraps from the table. She'll bring

161

off the whole brood for you . . . '

They expected no thanks. They were embarrassed by thanks. They just wanted the honour to take part in a miracle of God and that is absolute truth. It was their pleasure and they were great people . . . pioneers of the modern world, who knew the pleasure of being good neighbours.

We were able to give hospitality, but it was their own generosity. It all just happened by courtesy, the cooked ham and the fresh bread, the wedges of butter and cheese and the kegs of beer, the side of bacon, fresh killed pork . . . the cornucopia of plenty. Here was Southern Ireland at its best — a land as freshly reborn as Israel from its own ashes, and as old in civilization as ever Israel was.

So the fields were ploughed and planted by the lights of cars late into the night, after the work was done on their own farms. It was like a great harvest thanksgiving that went on, till the seed was set and the farm back in business . . . and all the reward anybody wanted was to see the Colleen Bawn and run a hand down her nose . . . She had a magic about her and she took all the glory in her stride . . . and sometimes I heard the story again.

One day an old woman crept round to the back door and was entertained by Rose and myself before the kitchen fire, because she would not be comfortable in the sitting-room, though we laughed her opinion about that to scorn.

'I recall your mother well, Miss Cordelia, as like her as two peas in a pod. She didn't care about being cut out of her inheritance ... The old lady saw to that with Lyre na Greana, but 'twas a poor place for a lady born to come to. It was the thought of what happened to the lovely mare. She knew that Bawn would fret after her and there was no way of tracing her. He's a hard master, Cormac, always was and always will be. Take care of Himself, Sister Mark. We all knew that God would never close His eyes to what Cormac did that day and wasn't it the end of all happiness for him? Doesn't it put the faith in your breast, the way God done it at the finish — the second Cordelia back again, as like her mother as ever a daughter was? Och! There has been nothing like it to happen here for a hundred years. He done it in His own time. They say His mills grind small. We're all that glad to be part of what He wanted to come about, that maybe never would be heard of ... and maybe no importance at all ... but it has to us.'

Rose and I gave her tea before the blazing stove and we were all very happy in a crazy

163

sort of way. She took down the green plates off the dresser and washed them and put them up again and delighted to do it. She had been a kitchen maid in the old days and she felt youth again . . . and we loved her and so she went away, with a cake Rose had baked and all our good wishes and she knew she was part of 'the miracle' . . . and indeed she was.

I do not know how it was done, but done it was . . . and the soft Irish voices a background to it all . . . and laughter and happiness again.

Perpetually there was tea and home-made soda bread and butter and jam on the kitchen table and fried bacon and eggs, as much as anybody might want, if the hunger came on them . . . and a keg of beer always on tap for the thirsty ones.

There were so many of them, going and coming, sometimes tired after their own work. I could not turn around, but a task would be done. I went out to the milking one evening and stopped to talk to a young woman, who was whitewashing the kitchen. By the time I had finished my chores, the kitchen was like a new place, the floor scrubbed white stones . . . even the old clock started again with its swinging weights and chains. It was like no world I had ever inhabited. They were all faceless and maybe they were angels, for their impeccable behaviour, but I do not think they were, any more than Michael was an archangel. Yet still I did not know who had sent him . . . and he had been the forerunner of them all.

It destroyed Cormac. I saw it happen with my own eyes. He grew old and diminished and dwindled down and wandered to senility. Mostly he thought I was Cordelia, Mark one, but the past was wiped out of his brain. He was indeed the feeble, fond, old man of Shakepeare . . . and he had forgotten the delights of alcohol. He had forgotten everything . . . his hate and his spite and his cruelty. He was Cormac of Cormac's Castle, stripped of all rank, with all venom gone.

I thought uneasily of my outcry against God on the cliff top. Surely He had not taken heed of what was only a hysterical outburst? But if He had, who was Michael Grant, who had told me he was a sort of hybrid archangel? I had gone no further in solving the mystery of Michael. Every time I turned my thoughts to the solving of Michael's identity, a crisis arose on the farm. The sow was 'on the point of lay' as Rose put it one day and that meant that we had fourteen bonhams and not enough 'faucets', so that we had two little pigs, one at either side of the kitchen hearth, to bring up on the bottle. I might get back to wondering, who 'had sent Michael', for he had more or less said that to me himself, but always something turned my thoughts off. It might be Rose, who appeared in distress, because her husband was too genteel to approach a lady with such things.

'There's a man come with the bull. I don't know what to do with him. Can you tell me, Sister? In the old days, I never had anything to do with the outside work, but things are going to the devil these times, with yourself polishing floors and forking muck. I daresay, we'll have the yard man waiting on table at any moment.'

I knew exaltation one day, as I leaned on the sty door, and scratched the back of the young pigs with an ash plant.

'I don't know how you manage them,' Michael said at my side. 'I'd been chasing them round the yard for twenty minutes and I couldn't corner them . . . '

Not the Archangel Michael! I thought and told him that he only had to have a pocket full of little apples, but then how could an archangel know a thing like that.

'A lady of great expertise,' he smiled at me. 'I never met one like you. I saw you that first night in your green velvet dress and I think I'd dreamed about you all my life. Now I see you in fatigue denims and smelling of pig and you're more beautiful than ever.'

He laid a hand on my shoulder and said it was not the time or the place, because it was the thing to put such moments in the family bible and press sweet flowers on the same page . . . tell your children's children about it.

'It's all wrong, but I can't help it.'

He took a deep breath and let it out slowly, and his face was strained.

'I love you and I'll never stop loving you, I don't know if I can ever walk the world again. I may disappear in the blink of an eyelid . . . be nobody, with no chance of ever finding you again. It is possible. I must tell you once and for all, so that you'll know I warned you. It won't be my fault, but it is possible. Oh, God! This is no time nor place. I sent signals, but got no reply. I shouldn't even tell you that. They seem to have cut me adrift. Just remember that I told you I loved you, just because I wasn't able to stop myself. I walk in a place I never walked before and may never walk again. There's such happiness here with you, that I didn't believe possible.'

So I loved the Archangel Michael, I thought, but of course it was quite, quite out of the question. It always was. Archangels did not come staggering in out of the night,

clothed in olive drab and soaked to the skin
... with grazed chest and torn fingernails
... suffering from loss of memory, that
seemed to have gone on for a long time, or
perhaps not.

Oh, no! Things like that never happened,
but miracles did not happen either and a
miracle had happened here ... a sort of
'loaves and fishes miracle, Mark two' like
myself. Was I not Cordelia, Mark Two? It was
a strange coincidence.

6

Tinker . . . Tailor . . . Soldier . . . Sailor . . .

The doubts crept into my mind like slow toads. The first of them came the day Aunts Goneril and Regan came. Why can I never call them by their right names? They were Grace Craddock of Cashel Farm and Rosemary Louise Macauley of Lismore Farm and both of them *née* Cormac, but always I called them by the name Lear's wife had put on them at last, my grandmother, Constance Peppard. Let's leave them at that. They came together to get enough moral strength. They were ashamed, that the County had seen that they were not helping us and they were two ferrets come to nose out the stranger.

They had heard in town that we had a man staying here. They wanted to know all about it. As a Trojan horse, they brought a pound of Jersey cow's butter and half a sack of potatoes. Who was I, as Cormac's grand-daughter to spurn such gifts?

Cormac hardly seemed to recognize who they were. He had grown very vague recently.

'All my pretty chickens and their dam at

one fell swoop,' he said. 'Welcome home my eldest daughters, tho' false ye be.'

They spied round the castle like two mobile computer machines and they put a value on everything they saw. They appraised the new barns and they examined the sheds and the enclosures and told me that we had done well for beginners, but we'd learn by our own mistakes.

Still they were both outraged by the way our neighbours had rallied round to help us.

'It's a nice thing when Cormac's Castle has to accept charity, for that's what it is. You ought to think shame on yourself for making our father into a beggar. There was no need of it.' Regan said at last and then Goneril was after my trail.

'There's another thing. You've taken it on yourself to give hospitality to lodgers. They have it in town that a stranger came in from the cliff, and you hadn't the sense to turn him in to the Police or the County Hospital. We often wonder if you've any sense at all, the way you carry on. You're your ma all over again, but that's to be expected. Still, it was no right of yours to plant a total stranger as a guest in our father's house . . . with never a word to us.'

'That guest has been far more helpful to the farm, than either of you.'

It was unwise of me, but sometimes I can't curb my tongue.

'As to this queer fellow in the olive gear, likely he's a G.I. Joe on the run from the camp in the valley. How do you know he isn't? There's jail bird written all over him and they say he's grown a beard and that's to hide under. Don't say we didn't warn you! He'll make off one of these nights, do a moonlight flit and half the farm with him and you'll not see him again.'

'You'd better listen to me,' I said. 'Michael is a good man. I know it. You'd never believe the help he's given us here. We couldn't have existed without him. He'd taken a knock on the head and he doesn't remember much, but we're giving him time. It will all sort itself out in the finish.'

They looked at me disbelievingly and sneered a little.

'If you believe that, you'll believe anything. Mind he doesn't lift your character and the place too.'

'He helped us with what strength he had, when he was ill. He was marvellous, the way he put himself last. I swear he's a good man . . . '

I lost all patience with their tittle-tattle and I told them to get out. They took me at my word and flounced down the front steps.

It was no good coming to them for help, they said, if I had my throat cut.

I could only stand there and look at them and think of how stupid they were and I was very angry indeed and then I saw the funny side of it and began to laugh. It was petty . . . petty . . . petty . . . They had always acted true to form and they did so now. I must not let them get under my skin.

Then a week later, I saw something was missing from the kitchen . . . not anything of great importance, but it was gone, and with its disappearance came a small doubt, that was quite out of proportion.

I had a postcard on the kitchen mantelpiece, a picture of Cormac's Castle. It was behind the clock on the mantel-piece and I had bought it in the town, for it was an old photograph in colour of our castle and what it had been years ago. It was the sort of thing a tourist might buy. I asked Rose about it and she said it had probably been blown down and swept up with the ashes on the grate.

'There's plenty more where that came from. They sell them at the Post Office. Still, I'll bring you another next time I'm in town.'

'Did you see the missing postcard, Michael?' I asked him and there was a hesitation.

'I saw it, but it's not there now. It's of very

little value. Don't worry about it.'

'Did you take it, Michael?'

He gave me neither a 'yea' or a 'nay'.

'I'll bring you another from the town, if you set such value on it.'

Anyway why should he take a postcard? I tried to put it out of my mind, but it hung round and would not be forgotten . . . would not be written off.

Then the aunts called on me again and I took them through to the comfort of the kitchen, for I did not want to see them alone and I thought Rose might chaperon us, but she did no such thing. She went out through the door as they came in and said she'd get the tea, for she liked them no more than I did. Indeed, she was back again with tea on a trolley and small cakes and biscuits and I wondered how she did it, cut off from the kitchen stove.

I poured the tea from the best china and was glad that Rose now kept a Dundee cake in a tin 'against' unexpected visitors.

'We came because we thought you ought to know, Mark. We felt it our duty, though I don't know why we come here to be insulted. There's no doubt that your man here is up to no good. An extraordinary thing was called to our attention the other day and we thought it only fair to let you in on it. It's about that American G.I. Joe you have here working for you and living off the fat of the land . . . '

It made my ears tingle to listen to them, so much, I wanted to tell them to get out, but I held my peace, though I flamed with anger . . .

They had been in the Post Office in town the other day, since they'd seen me. They saw the man, whom I was harbouring 'in my bosom', posting a card in the Post Office box. They had watched him directly from the shop window.

'Mary Scully, the post woman, took it out for us, because we explained what was going on. It was that card you had on the mantelpiece. Have you got it now?'

I shook my head reluctantly and reminded them that there were dozens of the same postcard floating round the business world.

'You won't laugh when you hear the rest of it, Miss Kinsella!' Goneril said and I make no excuse not to call her my Aunt Grace.

'Mary Scully was put out that it was unstamped. That made us all wonder and she agreed with us. It wasn't right. She asked us to put a stamp on it, but why should we? Still it would have been worth it to get a look at that card and so we did . . . both of us.'

They sat there like two hunting bitches having retrieved one pheasant between them, and expecting praise. I sat silent and waited with my heart beating fast.

'It was the funniest thing you ever saw. There was no sense in it. It was addressed to a Mr. Byrne or Murphy or Joyce, or some Irish name. That's of no importance and we didn't get the address. It was somewhere in Cove, County Cork. It was that silly, we couldn't make much sense out of it.'

My mind fumed anger against them. They had seen the wretched thing and had made no accurate observations.

'It was all about Molly Malone . . . you know the song. Everybody knows it. Of course, we knew what it was, but there was something not quite right. It said

'In Dublin's fair city,
Where the girls are so pretty,'

Then it went on

'But the cockles and the mussels are
still alive, alive-o!

Note that Molly Malone is dead and gone.' We couldn't make a head or tail of it an really it's none of our business . . . '

Instinctively I covered up for him and I will never know why.

'You'd want to be a millionaire to be sending postcards these days,' Goneril was saying and in a split second of time, I wondered if I loved him, because of the way, without thinking I had shielded him.

'It's all right,' I laughed, offering a slice of the Dundee . . . calmly, or so I thought. 'He posted that card for me and he forgot the stamp. Trust a man to do that! I sent that card to a chap on Radio-therapy . . . one of the Registrars, who thought he was a funny man. Oh, dear! It's a long story, but it's hospital humour. You'd better hear it. There was another sister with me, a girl called Malone, and he thought it the peak of fun to christen us Cockles and Mussels. Don't ask me why. He couldn't pass one of us in the corridor, without humming it. In these places, if you don't laugh, you can't survive. I suppose it was his way of keeping us alive. Malone and I were glad to giggle sometimes. I give you my word, but you have no idea of the life you have to live there. If you don't laugh, you die with each patient and after a time, you're broken. It's an extraordinary artificial world of extraordinary values and there's a survival code . . . '

I laughed then and thought it a tolerably

good imitation of a laugh and somewhere in the back of my mind, I knew I could never take the strain of it again . . . not when I could go out to the stable at night and lean my face against the warm side of a little Kerry cow, under the warm light from the hurricane lamp.

The aunts had not uncovered high treason, I assured them, yet I wondered if they had. I walked them to the end of the avenue, for they had parked their cars there. I waved them goodbye and thanked them for their interest in me . . .

I walked slowly back along the avenue and I hummed the song.

'In Dublin's fair city,
Where the girls are so pretty.
I first set my eyes on sweet Molly Malone.
As she wheeled her wheelbarrow
Through streets broad and narrow
Singing cockles and mussels
Alive, alive O! . . . '

So Molly Malone had died, but her ghost lived on. There was no doubt that Michael had taken my card and posted it and it might mean anything. I should have poured the whole thing out to him, but I did not. If I had done it straight away, it was a mouse. Left, it grew into a mountain.

Metaphorically, I dug a hole and hid . . . marked it 'Observation only' like any trained sister, but from that day on, I watched him and I watched him unceasingly. It was a pity I closed myself away from him. If he could be secretive, then so could I.

There was something not quite right, but it could not hide out for ever, any more than a festering abscess. I waited and watched like any sister on special care and the mystery was slow in coming to light.

I withdrew myself from loving him, or thought I did. Although I worked at his side, there was a barrier between us.

The next clues came from O'Brien, with the evening paper in his hand, by the stove in the kitchen, one night.

'There's been a body washed up at the Old Head of Kinsale. They don't know who it is, but they have the Guards working on it . . . the Coast Guards. They have knowledge of how the tides run in these parts. They have it that the body went in near enough off our own cliffs yonder, but they're talking 'rubbitch'. There was nobody to go in off our cliff. We'd have known all about it. A man doesn't go in head-first off of that place, but we know all about it. To my mind, 'twill be some sailor man, off a ship at sea and drifted in to Kinsale.'

The friendly neighbours had taken themselves off, when they had set us on our way. We had one grand celebration night, when I wondered why they did not all fall off the cliff, for it was 'an Irish night'. As for me, I thanked God that Cormac turned away from the amber liquid, that had been his downfall. His eyes were sad and vague. He lived in a fugue.

'Drink up, my young masters, my fine young ladies, one and all, but never forget the devil it puts in your head to steal away your brains . . . and remember to decant Madeira for the ladies, or maybe elderberry wine, but I think the times are changing.'

The whole place was improved out of all recognition. The outbuildings were complete enough. The house was decorated. The barn was full. There were hens and ducks and geese walking the yard. There was big life about the whole place and again, I thought of an American musical and knew how they could put it over, this great resurgence.

Always in the back of my mind, recurred the thought that my duty was in Wentbridge. I had not solved the riddle of Michael. I had narrowed it down to three possibilities. Likely he was on the run from some situation in the north. That was my first choice. Then, he was no criminal. I was pretty convinced of that. He might be one of those extraordinary people from Interpol. It was over my head. Let's take a closer view, and wonder if Scotland Yard was after him. Yet he might be a criminal from any other country in the whole world and that gave me a vast choice, when I was convinced that he was not a criminal at all. He might have money hidden and have to lie hidden too . . . or might have come looking for it. I almost believed him an honest man and I thought there was a good chance that I had fallen in love with him. Of all the fool things!

I was quite sure that he had regained some of his memory, and had held out on me. In his delirium, he had spoken of lightning all the time. Was the storm at the nub of it all? There had been two storms, the first when I had thought to lift my anger against God and the second tempest that came on the heels of the first, or maybe, it was the same storm returned . . . what did it matter!

It seemed as if I might have started it myself and that was pure fantasy, the idea of the Almighty sending one of his great angels down to help me in my need, like the old priest, Father Gilligan. I recalled uneasily that Michael had said that he might not tread the world for long, or had he? Ideas were jumbling in my head. 'I am dead', Surely I remembered him saying that? Anyhow, who was I to presume that I could get such attention in heaven? I was no holy priest. I was Cordelia, the daughter of Cordelia, who had been disinherited by Cormac. My mother had died over a batch of home-made chocolates, meant for the shops of a small Irish town. Perhaps she had died, still breaking her heart for the Colleen Bawn, who was, at this moment, snatching at a mouthful of the fragrant sanfoin in her hay-net.

I had been reading the Guinness Book of Records. I had found it in the bookcase in the study, a copy dated 1968 on page 31 . . .

'The greatest acceptable age for a horse . . . is fifty-one years, for the ex-Italian Army horse, Topolino, foaled in Libya, on 24th. Feb. 1909. He died in Brescia, Italy in Feb. 1960 . . . '

I thought that there was a good chance of the Colleen Bawn being the white mare, most of them said she was. That was a miracle indeed. Why should there not be another, where God took pity on me, on my insignificant self, who stood on the edge of that tall windy cliff? There was no future in my wasting time, spying over what had happened here or had happened there, as my aunts always did. The farm was workable and there was plenty to be done. At night, I fell asleep before the kitchen stove, so tired that I had not the energy left to kick my wellingtons off, when I had bedded the animals down and turned out the storm-lantern. I would stagger to bed at last of course, but often after what seemed an hour or two, I might find an obstetric case on my hands. I was counted by the others, as the person of choice for the midwifery cases and indeed, I found a similarity between human obstetric and veterinary. A goat cried as a woman might, when her pains were strong. 'I can't go on any longer'. The goat might have been saying it too by that pitiful bleat. Then the kid would come diving out into clean straw, nose to front feet, if we were lucky, and the kid up on its feet in an instant . . . and the mother licking it. She would go back to licking it in with kind of fervour, if the afterbirth were long in coming. I sat on the rail of the enclosure one night and propounded the theory to Michael, that it might be worth researching, in cases of delay of the third stage of labour.

'Give the mother her baby to lick,' I suggested and he told me to take myself off to bed, before I fell asleep off the rail.

'In three hours, you'll be hard at work again, and you won't listen to reason. You'll say you must help with the milking and the separating and the churning. You're working too hard.'

The next day, in the afternoon, he took me off duty, with the authority of any sergeant major . . . told me I was resting far too little.

I forget what we were doing, but whatever it was, he assured me that John Joe and he could do it without me.

'Take the mare down the avenue. She'll follow you like a dog, but there's a halter, in case.'

He tossed it to me and for good measure, he put a handful of pony nuts in my pocket and said it was bribery and corruption.

'There's a green patch of grass by the trees at the front gate. It would be a treat for her and relaxation for you.'

The Colleen Bawn and I were very happy, as we sauntered along the avenue and the sun was shining. Now and again, she butted me in the back gently with her nose, as she clip-clopped daintily along. Sometimes, I stopped to let her crop some grass that was springing green against the good weather to come. At last, we reached the front gates and I went to look at the new gold-leafing of CORMAC'S CASTLE and was very pleased with it. Little by little, the pride of the house was returning. I loosed the halter and let the mare free in the green grass and she made the most of it. There was a fallen chestnut tree, that made a good seat for me to pipe dream. It was one of those magic days, when it seemed that winter was over and that spring had really come, but there was a while yet. It was all incredibly pleasant. Maybe I dozed off for a few moments. I must have done, for I was awakened by the sound of feet on the road outside . . . then the click of the latch of the gates. There was a man, who shut the gates carefully, stood with his back to me, viewing the range of mountains, stretched out before him. I had had a glimpse of his face and he had a grizzled beard and tufty brows, a cragged Scots face, a Sherlock Holmes hat and tweed knickerbockers, Norfolk jacket. A Scots gentleman, I thought, rather like that man on T.V . . . McDonald something or another, always on good programmes.

I was out of his sight behind some trees. I saw him through a gap in them, and unless he knew I was there, he could not have seen me. The Colleen Bawn was a hundred yards away. She had raised her head and was considering if there was any advantage in pushing her nose in his back. She decided that the grass was sweeter and presently, the stranger had started to sing in a pleasant baritone voice.

'In Dublin's fair city,
Where the girls are so pretty,
'twas there that I first saw sweet Mollie
Malone . . . '

I sat as still as a sugar mouse, but the voice interested the mare. The song was interrupted with the most gentle push in his back and a most ladylike nuzzle at his pockets and he spun round and his hand to her nose at once.

'Och! my beauty. Och! The grace and the loveliness in you . . . and what are you doing out here by yoursel'? Dinna they ken ye're loose, my lovely white girl?'

I stood up from my seat and went across to give him some of the pony nuts and he was very obliged to me, his hat in his hand at the sight of 'Mistress? Mistress? Mistress? . . . '

'Kinsella is my proper name but I never get it. They all call me Sister Mark hereabouts, or maybe Cordelia.'

'Cordelia?' he said. 'That's the name of a princess maybe or a queen. It suits ye fine.'

It gave him the greatest pleasure to feed the white mare and she made up to him, but he said she was fickle, for she went away when the food was done and took to grazing again and we laughed about it.

'Are you the mistress of the house then?'

I shook my head.

'I came over here to do some nursing.'

I left pause for a question and he told me at once that he was on a walking holiday.

'I got tired of the grand road from the mountain, that goes shining to the sea,' he said, and I finished his quote for him.

'I don't like it myself, nor the traffic in it and many a horse and cart. I suppose you're looking for the little roads of Cloonagh, to go rambling through your heart. You'll find them here, true enough. It's a lovely part of Ireland.'

He looked at me keenly and smiled, asked me if I would mind it, if he took out his pipe and polluted the air and again, I shook my head.

'You're the lassie for me!' he said and presently, we were sitting side by side on the fallen chestnut and he, with his pipe going well and the Colleen Bawn coming back to us like a playing child, a time or two, to see if any food had materialized.

I told him a deal of the story of the family and he was most interested in it. God knows! I was not one for gabbling, but there was something about this man, that drew out confidence. He knew Shakespeare well and all about King Lear and was enthralled to hear what had happened, that was so like King Lear's story. My tongue was loosed.

Perhaps it was time I told it all to a stranger. I certainly released some tension that afternoon and I have no excuse for it.

He heard about the white mare and how all the countryside had come to our side.

'She was a kind of a fiery cross . . . calling the people to war. They had the fiery cross to summon the clans in Scotland, but you'll know that?'

'I think maybe you won't have any more misfortune,' he said. 'You've had more than enough and these things average out. There must be many people who come this way, who would be glad to see over Cormac's Castle and would pay for the privilege. It's how people afford to live in castles these days . . . continue to keep them in their families.'

'We have no tourists. We're off the beaten track. I don't think anybody ever comes this way. The 'great road' by-passes us, for the little lanes, by good luck.'

'Aye! It's better that way.'

'You'd be welcome to walk with me along the avenue and see over the place. We had a young man come this way a while back, but he came by the back avenue, along the track from the cliff.'

Oh, I was a pigeon for the plucking, when it came to espionage, but I did not see it, did not even remember what had been written on the back of the postcard . . .

We made him very welcome and Rose fed him the home-made bread and the black-berry jelly and good hot strong tea. He was delighted with us. The talk of what had gone on went over and over and only Michael worried that all work had come to a stand still. At last, he offered to see our guest on his way. I said I might go with them, but Michael rode me off that.

'You're out on your feet, Mark. Please take it easy. You're killing yourself with this blasted farm. You'll be dead, if you don't stop it. Do you hear me? You'll be dead. Then see what thanks anybody gives you.'

It struck me with the force of a bomb. I would be dead, but Mollie Malone was dead. It was what had been written on the back of the postcard and I had forgotten it . . . had not connected it with the stranger's song today. I can only say I was very tired that afternoon, but that's no excuse.

I watched them walk off down the avenue, their two heads together in conversation. How could I have been such a fool, as to miss? This man had come in to Michael's call on the postcard without a stamp. It fitted too well. It could not be such a coincidence that he sang that song. There were other people in the plot, but maybe this was the head man, the camouflaged stranger walking in land that made him a chameleon, so like bonnie Scotland it was. God! It could mean anything. This might be the top man arriving with Michael's share of the loot. It was fantastic but it was possible. This man was no stranger to Michael. Michael had not even bothered to be polite and welcome him, while the rest of us were fussing about him like bears about honey. It was such a lonely place that we maybe overwelcomed the passer-by, but not Michael. He had wanted the business done and the man away. I had thought him jealous of the attention the stranger paid to me, silly ass that I was. Michael wanted him safely away.

I took to my heels and I ran as fast as I could, along the short cut to the gates. If they could play at spies, then so could I. I got to the gates, five minutes before they did, panting and not in any way tired, for the way the blood coursed my body. I must have cover. I found it behind a gorse bush, that prickled me for my pains, but it was right up against Castle Cormac gates, and this time I heard the click of the latch out and the click of the latch in.

I had no shame to eavesdrop. Michael might have confided in me. He had not done so. He must take the consequences that I was a splinter party. I was on my own and mighty mad with him, but full of excitement and curiosity, as bad as my aunts ever were. Why must I alway see both sides of an argument? It was a great disadvantage to morale . . .

'It was an act of God, laddie. Nobody could have foreseen it. You killed him, but we'll have him up again. We'll send down divers for good measure. Have you thought that you could live here for the rest of your life? You're invisible here and you should continue so to be. You'll be put out to grass, by their lordships, like an old horse. You'll have a generous pension for your services, but you're no use to us any more. There will be a very golden handshake, and if you're interested, it's in my mind, the lassie's in love with you. She has been taken with you since the first day you walked into her life. She's had no time to know men. Yet, she has a most profound knowledge of mankind. Always, she has given and never once looked for rewards. *Here is no clock-watcher, Michael.* Here is a fine lassie, who deserves her happiness, and I think you hold it in the palm of your hand. You could live here for the rest of your days and breed sons by her, breed white horses if you wish, but this place could be paradise.'

'This is John James Benedict Cormac's Castle,' Michael said. 'Lear is a hard unscrupulous man.'

'You've played your part. It's time you were off-stage. My! Was I glad to get that card, when I thought there was no more to you . . . thought your bones were of coral made. These were pearls that were your eyes . . . and all in the call of duty. You've gone *beyond* the call of duty, laddie. Put out your hand and pluck the reward. I doubt you'll get medals for this. It's all hush-hush, and nobody to say one word, except that you're dead and gone.'

I felt weak and sick. Michael had done murder. Here was intrigue at high levels and I was mixed up in it, knowing nothing about it . . . only that 'for Michael read Cain'. Now it was time to run as hard as I could to reach the castle before Cain reached it, but I was on guard now. That was the difference.

'Contact Cove again, if anything blows up.'

I was on my feet again, running like a rabbit for the comfort of the kitchen and Rose. I had felt weak and sick, as I listened to the shod feet on the road outside. I ran till my lungs were near to bursting and thought how they had contrived at something, the planners the tricksters. My world was no longer the bright place it had been. He had not trusted me enough to tell me, and me dressing his wounds, twice a day . . . and me bathing his forehead with cold water and his hands with eau de Cologne.

Presently he came in as cool as a cucumber and put a jacket into my lap, having just told me that I was overworked. He had a button in his other hand.

'I've lost a button. At least, I haven't lost it. I found it. Could you sew it on for me.?'

I sewed on the button slowly, and picked a time and went through his pockets as well. This was how a spy must behave. In the jacket pocket, I found a thousand pounds or thereabouts in used notes and I bit my lower lip till it bled . . . gave him the jacket back and half hated him.

He came to me at my desk later, thrust a bundle of notes into my hands.

'It's yours, Mark. I owe you a deal more, but you're to take this for now. Don't kill yourself scrimping on this place. Take the money and use it. Don't go scraping the bottom of the barrel till you've knocked yourself up, to save people who are maybe not worth the saving.'

I looked at him coolly and shook my head, but still he persisted. I took the money, put it into a drawer in the desk and turned a key on it, handed the key into his hand. He looked at me sadly.

'Don't doubt me, Mark. Never doubt me.

Only start to love me a little. Times are difficult. I'm lonely and maybe a little afraid. Please have faith in me.'

I said nothing, just sat there with my head down. I did not believe him. I did not trust him. There was only one thing I was sure of. No matter what he had done, I loved him. There was no use my denying it to myself. I would love him till the day either he or I died and possibly on down the years from that. There was nothing I was not prepared to do to help him and that was an inescapable fact.

I shut up the desk again and he sat there, turning the key in his hands. I looked at the scarred finger-tips and soon the nails would have grown again and nobody would have known his suffering . . . only he and I perhaps, given luck, Rose O'Brien and her husband — and John Joe . . .

He put the key into his pocket carelessly and I took his hands in mine again and ran my fingers along the young nails.

'What did you do to gain these, Michael? They'll soon be healed and perhaps you'll forget what happened, but what did you do to earn them?'

He laughed at that.

'It was well worth it. It saved my life for me.'

'Was it worth such agony, Michael?'

He left his hands in mine and looked me straight in the eye.

'They saved my life,' he said again. 'It was well worth it.'

'Was it for me, Michael?' I asked him and he denied that at once.

'I hadn't even met you. In the sense that you're part of mankind then I suppose it was for you and many others too. It was the way it was set up and you'll decide one day. Just for now, it's best you know nothing about it. I'm a dead man and I'll never be anything else. They counted me expendable . . . '

There was hurt to his pride here and pain in it.

'Maybe I'll never come near to finding you on your own level. I can't come to life any more . . . having been seen to be dead, beyond all possible doubt.'

He retrieved his hands from mine and stood up, pressed his lips against my forehead and consumed me again with fire. There came again the sensation that here was no real person, but somebody, who had come directly from God. I had done Michael most grievous wrong in doubting a word he said, but perhaps, yes, almost surely, I was crazy and it was all my fantasy.

How could a woman fall in love with the Archangel Michael? Yet it seemed in that space of time, that it might have happened to me. That night I had a fearsome dream, that woke me with sweat on my brow, with sweat drenching my whole body.

There was a man, who was dead, beyond all doubt, yet in my dream, I knew that he was not dead. I knew I had to lay him in his coffin. I knew that men would come for him. They would put the coffin in the sea and float it out with the tide and there was nothing he could do or say, just let himself be sent out on the ebbing tide and presently sink to the bottom of the depths and see the water come bubbling in through the cracks in the coffin, till it invaded him and made him truly dead . . . a thing of the most awful horror.

I was glad when the day came. I got up before time and started the milking, glad of the warmth of the byre against the winter. I leaned my head against the flank of one of the little Kerry cows and thought my hair was as dark as hers, but it was better to think as dark as a raven . . . not as a Kerry cow. I stopped off on the way into the kitchen with the milk, to talk to the Colleen Bawn . . . came back with her hay-net and her bran and chaff and a few handfuls of oats in it . . . a little sugar cake, that I had stolen for her from the tin in the kitchen. We had a long conversation that morning and she was very pleased with me. I took the fork and cleaned out the stable, spread half a bale of fresh straw round the cobbles and knew that maybe I would settle to this work for the rest of my life, but, but, but . . .

Rose had breakfast ready on the kitchen table and I was hungry . . . a bowl of cornflakes, fried eggs and bacon and home-made soda bread, with our own butter . . . and nobody there but myself and Rose, for the others had got up even earlier than I . . .

'Do you remember in the paper, the other day about the body that was lifted from the sea at the Old Head of Kinsale?' she said and I knew by her that she was full of gossip and bursting to unload it.

'They said they thought he went into the sea off the coast here,' she went on, and started to keep me in suspense.

'Maybe the Coast Guards had the right of it . . . ' she continued. 'They're used to the currents. They could tell you within half a mile where a body went in and where it must come up. They have great learning.'

She paused and I said nothing and presently she filled it in. 'The boy was here with the papers. He had it all.'

There was a grapevine in the district, that spread news faster than any medium. Rose was delighted to be able to tell me that the Irish Navy was interested in the dead man. Something was going to happen. Investigations were to be made official. Rose hoped that they did not come nosing round the castle, for we had done too much entertaining of late.

'Anyway, what could we tell them, Miss Mark?'

'What indeed?' I echoed, and thought of 'the dreary dream' of last night.

I was very unhappy. I was in the centre of a whirlpool of intrigue and I could see no way of ever being free of its whirling water. I can never bear the strain of something secret ... some silent animosity against another person. I stuck it all day and then cornered Michael in the stable that evening, where he had gone to bed down the white mare. He was feeding her bits of bread roll and biscuits. Another time I would have asked him if Rose knew he had been at the biscuit tin, but there was a barrier between us.

'Michael, will you tell me one thing? Did you whistle up that Scotsman, with a postcard that you took from the mantelpiece and posted without a stamp to an address in Cove?'

He looked surprised for a moment and then tried to make light of it, apologized for taking the card and told me he was not aware I was a master spy and how had I found out.'

'The post mistress saw you do it. She took the card out of the box and saw it had no stamp. She read it and then she showed it to my aunts.'

He was amused by it. He said that was how battles were lost. How could he realize that I had a spy-ring in the parish? Actually he had not had the money to buy the stamp and that had been a nice carry-on, for an important mission.

Always this was the way he laughed at me, as if I were a little girl. I determined to prick his sureness of himself.

'Actually I know what you wrote on that postcard. You wrote some of the verse of 'Molly Malone' on that card, sent to a man in Cove. You said . . . I quote, 'But the cockles and mussels were alive alive oh! even though Mollie Malone was dead'. You posted it without a stamp and in a very short time, a man appeared at the gates of Cormac Castle, with the same song on his lips. I intercepted him by accident, but later, I heard him speaking to you. I eavesdropped, if you like to put it like that. I know that there's something of vast importance . . . going on and I'm outside it.'

'You've got a very good espionage system,' he said.

There was little worry about him, but then confidence tricksters work like that.

There was a pile of baled straw in the stable and he put his arms under my elbows and lifted me up, imprisoned me with a hand on either side of me and stood looking up at me for a long time till the Colleen Bawn whickered from her loose box for one of us to come and pay attention to her need for scraps from table. He took no notice of her, just looked to see that the hurricane lamp was burning safely. There was the warm stable smell all about us.

'Do you remember now who you are?' I shot at him. 'It's been forgotten for weeks, with all the building up of the Castle farm, but it's an important issue. I think maybe you've remembered the whole of it now.'

'I remember the most of it . . . a bit misty in parts, but that man, who called, filled me in on the vague bits. Things have gone fairly well, but there's more to come. I'm incommunicado.'

He smiled at me and thought that I ought to understand what he meant, if I was so skilled in the art of the spy-ring.

I was angry with him. It was no childish game to me, but a matter as important as any

I had had to settle before. He saw I was upset and was gentle with me.

'You've blundered into a very dangerous world. It's no part of you. You're no part of it. Otherwise, I'd never have heard of Sister Mark, of Wentbridge General.'

I frowned down at him and he put up his hands and took a plait of my hair in each hand, as they lay along my shoulders.

'I'm bound by honour not to reveal any part of this thing . . . I've given my oath and my loyalty. I'd be glad if you'd give me your faith. I want you to come to love me and marry me, if time lasts the thing out. It may all go to bits under us even now, but I don't think it will. I shoved a scheme in the right direction, but it didn't stay that way. There's an end game . . . '

'You expect me to marry you, not knowing who you are or what your name is. There's no doubt now, that you're no archangel, Michael. Can't you even tell me your name?'

'My name is Michael France,' he said moodily, 'But that clue won't help you . . . rather the reverse. It's a very tangled web.'

I had him quickly on that one.

'We weave tangled webs when we deceive. Michael France. In the choice of husbands, I'd never buy a pig in a poke.'

'Charming,' he said and laughed . . . told

me that I was nothing if not honest, but I was not an easy woman to woo.

'So you want to woo me?' I said with sarcasm. 'You're going a strange way about it.'

We parted moderate friends, still with me thinking that almost surely I was being had for a fool.

'If you loved me you'd trust me,' I said and he asked me if I had never heard of Mata Hari. He was far too light-hearted about the whole thing to be a villain, but I doubted him. A man can smile and smile and be a villain.

In the morning, there was more detail in the National Press about the body that had been washed up at the Old Head of Kinsale. There had been an inquest held at Kinsale Hospital and a positive identification made. The body was that of a senior British Naval Officer, Michael Gatling.

Some fragments of uniform had been found and also a waterproof wallet, which provided precise details. He had held a high rank in the British Navy and he had been involved with United Nations. The findings at post-mortem examination were being checked against known details of Captain Gatling's files, in the British forces.

The inquest was put off *sine die*, pending further investigations. The Civic Guards from

Munster would liaise with officers from England, to enquire into the circumstances of death but there was no reason to suspect foul play.

Captain Gatling had an excellent service record. Almost certainly, his death had been the result of some tragic accident . . .

About this time, we were diverted from the subject by Cormac, who was becoming increasingly fragile in health, increasingly unstable mentally. I would have counted it senile degeneration, but that was a hard diagnosis for anybody to make. Yet, he had taken to wandering if we did not watch him. He would be found in the twilight, going along the avenue to meet Constance Peppard returning from the market town. Maybe he would be up on the hills after the sheep. Then the next minute, he would be lucid and sensible. He was constantly harassed in his mind about the Colleen Bawn.

'I did wrong to take the mare away from the girl. Cordelia thought the sun, moon and seven stars shone out of her . . . and Bawn followed her round like a dog follows his master. I can't understand it, how she found her way home, but she's in the same loose box this minute, but Cordelia's in her grave, isn't she? I can't recall an odd time. Is Cordelia, my daughter, dead? Maybe I dreamt it? Are you my daughter, Cordelia?'

He would worry about the Hunt Supper that night, when Hunt suppers were a thing of the past. He spent a great deal of time in the stables, making much of the white mare, talking to her, as if she could understand every word he said ... all a jumble of the days gone by and no sense in his words ... grasshoppering the generations. I think what was left of his mind was grieving with remorse for what he had done and could never undo. At least that was how I saw it.

To me, he was an additional burden on the estate ... somebody who had to be watched, sheep-dogged, saved from harm, but there was so much work to be done, that it put us to the pin of our collars to watch him carefully. I was full of guilt myself for my impatience with him, but I knew he lived in hazard, as all senile people do ... tried to tell myself we could only do what was possible. In the back of my mind, hung the fears.

He had only to have a fall, a long wandering out of civilization to somewhere, he might not be found on a cold night. He wore all our nerves to tatters, but still he was the master of the castle. Still he was Cormac. We could not shut him up in an old person's home. It would be like sending him to prison, this Lord of the Castle ... as soon send him to the workhouse, if there had been such a place, or back to school. He had to have what happiness was left to him, though I imagined it was very little and maybe misted by strange fancies. We saw he had respect and love and we felt grateful that by some kindness of God's he had forgotten the delights of alcohol. At least, that plugged the waste, that had run away with income. We could edge forward to success now.

So there he was, wandering about in a mazy dream. He had only to call out . . . one of us would be at his side . . . not able to stop loving for the more than life-sized figure he was. It is hard to understand, but it was so. He had wrought havoc, but he was still Cormac and his hand would stroke my hair and I was Cordelia, Mark one, all over again and he would tell me I must have a pony to ride. The next fair, he would buy one for sure . . . just the same as a galloper on the roundabout. If I liked, I could have a green velvet riding habit and a hat with a feather and sit side-saddle, like a grownup lady . . . and he would take me out alongside his black stallion, Sultan, but I must go on a leading rein . . .

John Joe found him dead by Constance Peppard's grave one day and it is no good to go back over the unpleasantness of his death.

It all ran to form. There was no neglect. He had gone out early on a spring morning, had knelt down and died. He had been looking for Cordelia's grave. It was one of the things he did habitually . . . asking why was his daughter not sleeping at home. We had grown accustomed to it, but we had not noticed him go out that morning. He had not long been dead and there was no difficulty about death certification. His heart had failed and that was it, what people call 'a happy release'. I felt a great poignancy, but no real regrets for him. His end was swift and merciful . . . a finish, that had spared him worse senility. His remorse had weighed him down and the knowledge that he could never put right a wrong.

This was Ireland, so the funeral was as impressive, as it might have been in Victorian England. There was a service in the town, that packed the church to the doors. There was a *cortège* with cars behind the hearse, that wound out to the open gates with the new gold paint . . . on along the twisty avenue. The people walked up the path to the graveyard. The aunts took charge of everything, as was their right as Cormac's daughters. They seemed to enjoy a great show of grief, in smart black suits and mourning veils, their husbands by their sides to support them and a great show of little white lace handkerchiefs.

I think all the countryside came to pay their last respects. These were the people, who had come to help us get the farm on its feet again. They were hardly recognizable in sombre suits and black ties, from the jolly pioneers from the mid-west, who had arrived in jeans and sweaters like an American musical show. There was such silence over us all.

'Lord, grant him eternal rest . . .
And let perpetual peace shine upon him.
May he rest in peace . . . Amen.'

The murmuring of the voices stole towards heaven and our faces were very serious and sad. Then it was over and we were coming down the hill. The hospitality was lavish. It was essential for the funeral of John James Benedict Cormac and many orations about what a loved man he had been.

I might have wished for a simple service at the small plot with the iron railings, with just the household present, but it would never have done, just to lay him to rest gently.

By the time the last guests were going, I was tired and remorseful too, wondering if I had given Cormac short change.

I had said goodbye to them and my hand was aching with shaking theirs. Now O'Toole, the solicitor had come over to the family.

'It's time for the reading of the will. Mrs. O'Brien has cleared the dining-room table and she'll be there and her husband and John Joe Fitzpatrick . . . yourself too, Sister Mark. We mustn't leave you out.'

He turned to the two aunts and said that they would not be required to be present, but of course, they had that privilege if they so wished. There was quick tension and a preparation for trouble.

'Only the beneficiaries need be there . . . '

The aunts would stay and it was their right to be there . . . their husbands too, but there was anger in their red cheeks already, so that I grabbed Michael by the arm and took him with me . . .

We sat round the dining-room table with the sherry decanter on a round brass tray and a glass by the side of each of us. I remembered Grandfather's insistence, that day, long ago, that the port be passed clockwise and wondered if he had reached a place, where such things had no importance any more. The solicitor had intimated that I was to be a beneficiary and I remembered some foolish talk from my grandfather, of how, when he was gone, I was to be an heiress in my own right, but I had paid no attention to it. Now I just wanted the whole thing over — signed, sealed and delivered, as they say, and now indeed the seal was broken and the red wax scattered down on the high polish of the mahogany table . . .

'Here then is the last will and testament of the deceased, John James Benedict Cormac of the residence known as Cormac's Castle in the County of Cork in the province of Munster in Southern Ireland . . . '

The solicitor had an old man's reedy voice and it was all the usual jargon and I was interested not at all. Here was my delivery from Cormac's Castle and all my duty there. Soon I could spread my wings and be away across the sea to the east.

'Being of sound mind, I make my will . . . written down in this document . . . and I appoint my solicitor as my executor, for I have trusted him for many years and will trust him, past the grave, when God calls me . . . '

It took me a time to absorb what the solicitor was reading out. The red chips of the sealing-wax were bright in the light, dramatic as blood against the shine of the mahogany of the table top. I could not understand what Cormac had done, and my mother just dead.

Maybe he had said to me that it would all

be mine one day, but I had not believed him. The will had been made not long after Cordelia, my mother's death, and it cancelled out all previous wills made by him.

John James Benedict Cormac had left the whole property to his granddaughter, Cordelia, lock, stock and barrel, it was to be mine, .. all the land, all the buildings thereon, all the contents thereof, all the livestock . . . the entire farm. It was lawyer's jargon, all signing and sealing. Still the sealing wax was blood on the table. I sat there and could not believe my ears. My whole life was being turned upside down, when I only wanted to be rid of my responsibility here and to get back to Wentbridge, or did I?

There were other minor bequests . . . five hundred pounds to Rose . . . the same to O'Brien her husband, the same to any employee in his service on the day of his death, and that was now John Joe.

I put my head in my hands on the table and then all hell broke loose, but I have no idea of putting down here the things that were said. The aunts were almost insane with anger and their tongues knew no silence about things that should never be said. Michael kept his hand on my arm and O'Toole, the solicitor, packed up his parchments and got out quickly.

'You'll do no good opposing this, ladies. The master knew what he was about the day he signed this document. The estate owed his youngest daughter a great debt . . . something he could never repay, for she was dead. I think maybe he's paid his debt in full today. I pray God he has done just that . . . He counted that you had already had your inheritance in very generous dowries, on the day of your marriage.'

He took leave of me and held my hand in his. 'He's at rest now, Cordelia. For your mother's sake, make it work out for him.'

They were all gone and after supper, I sat at my desk and tried to get my mind straight. If I turned away from Wentbridge, we could make this farm successful, Michael and I. I thought back to the man, who had come along the back avenue, that night, with Michael Grant on a tab on his G.I. shirt. His fingernails had been torn and his chest bleeding, his temple cut deeply. He had had almost complete amnesia from that cut and he had been a man from nowhere. I remembered Captain Gatling, taken from the sea of the old Head of Kinsale.

That night, I sent off a letter to 'the Proff' in Wentbridge. Perhaps, I have not made it clear that he and I had a regular correspondence with each other. I had kept him alive as to the affairs of the farm and just as regularly, he had written back to me in his sprawling writing telling me all the details of the Radio-Therapy Department. His letters were maybe the high spot of a week. Sister Tucker was ill, but I was not to worry. They missed her on the wards, but she would soon be back again. Jennifer Camps was getting married and he was delighted. Now she would have children and be a good mother, but she would be missed in the department. Janet Peck had been moved up to 'Computer controls', a kind of office job. Whoever heard of such a nonsensical idea, when she was the best material for practical nursing? Why did they always pick the best to sit behind a desk? There was no doubt that administration was all poppycock . . .

So now, I wrote and told him about Cormac's will . . . told him what had happened about Michael too . . . about the arrival of the strange man at the gate and 'Cockles and Mussels . . . ' I told him some of what I have put down here, things I had not confided before. I wanted to go and see him and ask him what to do, but I could not presume to do that. Besides, I did not want to leave my castle. Put like that, it seemed impossible, but I sent the letter off to him

... and Michael, knowing I was now an heiress, drew off his attentions a little ... imperceptibly, but quite definitely, and that upset me.

I have never been so uncertain in all my life, of what to do. I decided to live from one day to the next and see what happened and I had not long to wait.

Guard Sheehan, my old friend, who had brought the Colleen Bawn on the day of the fair, drove up in the Guards' car a few days after the funeral, about some unimportant detail or another. I forget what it was now. This was Ireland and there was a warm fire in the grate and a rocking-chair and a pint of Guinness by his hand and some of Rose's crusty home-made bread and cheese, which he liked very much.

'We've had great excitement below at the barracks,' he told us, as soon as we had got past all the talk of the funeral and my legacy, and what a grand old man the master had been, even if he had been a bit sharp in his judgements in his young days. 'But age gentled him, as it does many a man. Maybe the mistakes coming home to roost on the end of his bed, nights, made him wiser with the years ... older and wiser ... isn't it always the way?'

Then we heard about the body, that had

been taken from the sea off the Old Head of Kinsale.

'They've moved the enquiry over here. They've elected me a kind of a 'Deputy Coroner's Officer'. There's a strong current running out to sea from the bottom of the cliffs here. You throw a corked bottle in off the top of your cliff and in a week or two, maybe for longer, it will be bobbing up out of the sea at Kinsale, like as not. So now, it's our business and they sent a chap over from England specially, for they set great store by Captain Gatling. This fella came to the barracks to see me, for they have evidence of what happened to the deceased in the last hours before his death. It happened the second night of the storm, not the first night, but you'll recall the way it came back again, when we thought ourselves shut of it. I took this English chap out to the cliff . . . told him you've no objection, as long as he didn't fall over the edge. Did I tell you this Captain Gatling was stationed at the British Navy Depot across the valley from the hill south?'

Michael was sitting across the fire from the guard, with a cobbler's glove on his hand, trying to stitch harness and making a hard job of it. At this point, he stuck the needle into his hand and refused to let me fuss about dressing it . . . sucked at it and frowned and told the sergeant to go on with his story, before my eyes came out on stalks.

I tried to explain to him what a punctured wound can do and he laughed and advised me to stop behaving like a nursing sister. The guard was very amused with the backchat between us, but at last he went on with his account.

'They have evidence that Captain Gatling checked out of the depot that night on his way along the coast. Wasn't it a dark night, as dark as a dog's mouth? He knew the country, but not well. God rest him! It was easy done. He must have taken the turn up the cliff road. It's as like as damn it to the turn along by the coast. The storm didn't help him much, for it came on strong. We think it caught him up, as he reached the edge of the cliff and swept him over the way a goose's wing might have done. They want to know if the car is in the sea there. They're going to have a look anyway. He was a high-up fella in the United Nations . . . at the top of his trade, but I don't suppose that's how they'd describe him, the U.K. Navy crowd. They're very strait-laced. All this other man said was that he was 'of international importance', whatever good it does him now.'

'It's a long drop to the sea from those cliffs,' I shivered.

'They're planning to send men down the same cliff on ropes, climbing all over the place like spiders on a web. They'll be after marks of the car going over, but it's my opinion, they'll come on nothing more than gull's eggs and God pity them if the gulls take objection to them! They're very thorough, very thorough these chaps. It comes out that the captain was very important in the diplomatic . . . that he could sway the whole world with his 'Yea' or his 'Nay'. Let's hope he has the same ease to be swaying the courts of heaven.'

I saw the sergeant out into the cold drizzling rain and was worried to find where my thoughts were heading. I had heard Michael confess to the stranger that he had done murder, but it had not registered in my brain, not really. Now I thought that there might have been truth in what he said. That laird at the avenue gates, the man who had sung 'cockles and mussels', must have been some sort of agent. Come to that, it might have . . . it must have been a pass-word . . . and where did that leave Michael . . . this 'Cockles and Mussels?'

He had done murder, I thought now. It was possible that he had murdered Captain Gatling and pushed him and his car over the cliff. I was filled with uneasiness, uncertainty, conviction, and they grew like noxious weeds. It all fitted it. Michael might be in counter-espionage and who was I to know on which side he fought? If he was a villain, he had had an encounter on the cliff with Captain Gatling. It was possible that there were others involved and that Michael had been taken and tortured. Stranger things happened in modern times and his nails bore evidence of the most dreadful cruelty. Perhaps he had got away . . . had overcome Gatling . . . had sent him to his death and all the evidence with him.

The idea was ridiculous. I knew it, but that did not stop it growing like Jack's beanstalk. They had knocked Michael out with a blow to the temple. They had made him prisoner. They had questioned him and somehow he had got away, but there was too much at stake to let Gatling live. This was all television drama and could never happen out on the Castle Cormac cliffs and I knew it, but my brain would not accept the impossibility of it. The idea gnawed at me like a rat. After all, with my own ears, I had heard Michael say he had committed murder, yet a person might say 'I'll murder you', and mean nothing of the sort. What mother in the slums of Dublin has not threatened her child that 'if he did not come in out of the street, she would murder him?'

The words went round and round my head.

'It was an act of God, laddie. Nobody could have foreseen it. You killed him, but we'll have him up again'.

It sent my mind screaming up the skies. Murder was murder, was murder. Gatling must have been a good man. What did I know about anything at this level? I did not belong. Here was a man, who wanted to marry me . . . 'to marry a pig in a poke' and when I had said that, he had laughed and said 'Charming, I'm sure'. This was not the man I wanted to cleave to for the rest of my life, for better, for worse, for richer, for poorer, in sickness and in health . . . and all the rest of it. Better by far, for me to relinquish this fine new life of mine . . . to pack my bags and go. I would forget it all, settle in at Wentbridge, as if I had never left it. In a year or two, I would be married to one of the Registrars. I would bear him a son and maybe another son. Then I might find 'a substitute mum' to mind my babies . . . go back on the department and start my career off properly. It was what I always wanted . . . to be a career woman, but to have a family too and a happy marriage with a man, who spoke the same language as I did. It was what I had dreamed of since the first day I had put a foot inside Radio-therapy. It had been my whole life and I had been glad to have shucked off farming, but recently, I had grown back towards the country, and the warm smell of the stables in the evenings and the mists of the morning and the soft nose of the Colleen Bawn mesmerizing me to stay in Ireland and build up a line of white horses, that would vie with the white horses of Mannanan McLir, that rode the seven seas . . . then I saw myself for what I really was, a cold calculating woman, who weighed up marriage prospects, like a fishwife throwing mackerel into the scales.

There had been no answer from Went-bridge General to my letter, but often a month might pass before I heard from 'the Proff'. I took my pen and wrote the latest details to him, told him all about the new exciting developments and how I wanted his advice, as never I had wanted it before. He could consider the problem from a small distance and get the right angle. I was too close to it and I knew I was heavily biased.

Then one day, Guard Sheehan came again to check the pig records, though I thought it likely it was to sit in the chimney corner, where he was most welcome, just to drink Guinness and taste some of Rose's crusty homemade soda bread.

Guard Sheehan got more and more expansive, as the wag o' the wall went round its dial and the Guinness slid down the side of the glass. Still there was a drawing apart of Michael from, that I had noticed . . . the separation, the silence, the waiting. Still I did not trust him. I would not accept him without proof. I refused to shut my eyes to possibilities. Anyhow, how had he come by the awful injuries to his nails? Always that question popped up, over and over and over. Somebody had inflicted the most grievous torture on his finger nails.

Now it seemed to me that he went out of his way to avoid me. Yet perhaps he was determined not to be thought a fortune hunter. I had inherited what had every chance of being a successful farm.

He had tried to make me use the money that he had given me that night but it lay in the drawer or perhaps it did. He still had the key. He did not speak about it any more, but I had a suspicion that he was spending it. I had given him the key. I had no way of looking in the drawer. I thought that perhaps he had settled some of the accounts with it, or bought something necessary for the farm and no word to me. He was evasive about such things and there was an intangible mist, that grew higher and higher between him and me. It filled me with a desolation, that switched off the sun for me, that lovely May, when the whole County was as much a reflex of heaven as Killarney.

I had thought Cormac's Castle a cold gloomy fortress, but it had become a place of happiness . . . a golden land for lovers. Now I imagined that it was changing back again to greyness. It was eluding me, slipping through my fingers, the possibility of a happy ending.

I forced myself to concentrate on what Guard Sheehan had to say. He wiped the froth from his moustache with his usual blue handkerchief and got on with the gossip, and I tried to turn away from my personal thoughts.

Guard Sheehan had had notice that there were ships being sent over from England . . . British Naval vessels, two of them.

'The Irish Navy will be standing by to keep an eye on what's going on. The Super told me the English will probably send down a diver off one of the ships. It will coincide with the personnel out above on the cliffs. The Super told me about it, because I must be out on the top of the cliff. It's my duty as the local law. They had the decency to ask again if they could trespass on your land and of course, we said it was all right. We knew you wouldn't think anything of it. Beyond in England a man can't step on to another man's land without permission. It's a terrible way to go on. As I said to one of the fellas on the phone. It's a free country here. You can go anywhere between here and McGillicuddy's Reeks. You're welcome. You don't have to ask.'

I looked across at Michael, thinking to catch the reflection of laughter in his eyes, but he was frowning. He did not even smile, as the guard went on.

'It's deep down below there. There's a ledge of rock that'd break any ship's back and after that, it drops sheer, as deep as it soars to the skies above. They'll find nothing in the water but good fishing. If I had to be wrecked on a sea coast, 'tis not a place I'd choose. You'd be cut to ribbons, if there was a sea running and only the sheer cliff above you, reaching to heaven.'

He thanked Rose as she refilled his glass.

'It's a funny thing to say, but I mind when I was a little boy, I had great fear of those same cliffs of yours, Miss Mark. I thought and I really believed it, that if I wanted to talk to God, I had only to stand up there on the highest part of it all . . . and I'd meet Him face to face. The thought used to terrify me into good behaviour and the nuns in the convent told me I was probably right too. I avoided that old cliff for years and maybe it was as well. I was the kind of kid that couldn't go anywhere, without falling into something. The nuns were wise to leave me with that fear on me, that God would have me for certain, if ever I put a foot on the lane to the high place yonder.'

Michael was not amused, though I could have listened to Sheehan's rich County Cork accent in pleasure for hours. He was full of wit and humour and his voice was the musical singing of the deep south of Ireland. Michael was very ill at ease about something, but it was not obvious to anybody but myself, who seemed to think of nothing else, but this situation, that had been thrust on me.

'Why don't you both come up on the height and watch the operation?' the guard asked. 'It's to be in two days and they're starting at first light. We did think we found the place where a car might have gone over . . . the edge a bit jagged where it might have occurred . . . the sheep have been all over it ever since. They'll send some unfortunate 'Matlows' down on the end of a rope to have a closer look. It's strange the way the world turns, isn't it? If that was poor old Paddy Mooney, who took a drink too many of a Saturday night, and toppled over the edge, there'd have been no more about it. Let politics and nations have a hand in it and it's all of the utmost importance and everybody looking at everybody else out of the sides of their eyes, to see that might must prevail. What's more, it's my bet that St. Peter might be waiting at the gates of heaven with his hand stretched out to Paddy Mooney. For all you know, he mightn't even turn his head, when the great Michael Gatling came scratching to get in.'

Guard Sheehan I liked. I smiled to myself and then frowned for Michael had taken himself off to the stables, saying that he had a thousand and one things to do, but it was obvious to me that he had something on his mind and perhaps it was guilt.

As soon as the sergeant had driven off along the avenue, I pursued Michael to the stables, where I found him sitting on the manger, giving half slices of breakfast toast to the Colleen Bawn. I wasted no time about it. I have never been able to hand out diplomacy. I faced him squarely across the loose box and asked him if there was anything he wanted to tell me.

He shook his head and said no, slammed the door in my face metaphorically, and told me to mind my own business, but was it not my business? I pursued him and would not leave well enough alone.

'Are you afraid of what they're going to find out on the cliff?' I demanded.

He did not give me a direct answer to that, just stayed there, as still and as silent, as if he had been cut from stone. Then after a long time, he sighed and said 'No', and after a little he went on 'My conscience is perfectly clear.'

Still I couldn't leave it at that . . . challenged him again.

'All right then! We'll both go up there together and see what comes out of it.'

He looked at me for a silent twenty seconds, jumped down from the manger as if to walk away from me. Then he turned back, but reluctantly.

'Can't you bring yourself to have faith in me?'

I wheeled away from him and it was my turn to go now and no answer on my lips. I did not want to go, did not want ever to leave him in this life. If I had possessed wisdom, I knew it lost, as I turned back.

'But that night, that first night we met, you did come in along the lane from the cliff? It's the only way you can come from that direction. Therefore you had been on the cliff top and you were wet with either rain or sea-water . . . '

'Was I indeed?' he said and the ghost of a

smile on his lips. 'If it was sea-water, I'd been a long way down to get it.'

I knew myself unhappy, as unhappy as I had ever been. I knew myself deeply in love with him, ready to die for him, if it became necessary. I was not big enough to say it out to him that I loved him, right or wrong. I knew at last what uncertainty does to any poor animal specimen in the testing labs of the world.

He put out a hand and laid it on my shoulder to halt me. God help me, if his hand had carried high-voltage electricity, it could not have affected me more. I might have been struck by lightning, with the charge, that went through me from head to toe. If I had sparked like a November firework, I do not think I might have been surprised. If I had lit up like a high-powered electric bulb, it would not have seemed strange. The world was changing all about me. Here was a beautiful place. I had never seen it before. The colours were unbelievably clear and bright. The sky was an inverted bowl of blue sunshine. The birds were singing all together. The whole universe was singing. The flowers were in blossom. The honeysuckle in the hedge near the stable was incredibly sweet ... and it filled the whole air with sweetness.

'I did come in from the cliff top, but it was

only by the grace of God.' He paused, and he went on again. 'Listen to me Cordelia, and trust me blindly. There's tomorrow and tomorrow, two days. The navies are liaising and don't underrate Ireland. You're a prideful nation, but it's rightful pride. I imagine, that just now, what happened out there on the cliff, has been accurately assessed by both navies. They're going to clear this question up. They're determined to show the world what actually happened.'

He smiled at me and I knew him no evil man, thought I did. There was a devil's attraction in his line of beard and the tufts of his eyebrows . . .

'They are going to make sure of it. That's all it is . . . nothing more . . . It must be proved it was done . . . It must be seen to have been done.'

He took my hand in his and asked me if I would make an appointment with him.

'They're to start at first light, but they will take some time to get started. Let's see the sun rise together, in two days. Tomorrow, they're going to send down a diver and see what's there. There's a deal of drift with the current just under the cliff, where Sergeant Sheehan imagined he could contact God. If the chap finds anything, they'll bring out the derricks and we'll have it up. It all depends on the weather. One must never forget to take the weather into consideration.'

And could he be so sure of all that detail? I asked myself. He knew things that he could never have known . . . unless . . . unless . . .

I held his hand in mine and I whispered to him.

'I trust you, Michael. Right or wrong, I trust you. Let it lie like that and no more discussing it, this way and that . . . '

The waiting time was spent in a limbo of impossible politeness, strained almost to breaking. There was a storm inside me and I veered round the compass, from east to west to east to west. Sometimes all sense of direction left me and I spun to giddiness.

One minute, I was happy and it was May and the whole land was beautiful and the gorse was in bloom, but then it always is. I had never seen it bloom so splendidly, sending its peppery scent out to enclose the whole farm. Another minute and I was in despair. I was sick of the House of Jackdaws. I would take the next train back to Wentbridge . . . but I did not want to go to Wentbridge ever again, and 'this was none of I'.

Who was Michael and what part had he in my life? Was he a starting stick for the jackdaw's nest. Would he take the strain of the building of a life?

The countryside was at its loveliest. Looking to the north, you could see the range of mountains in every colour of the spectrum. The small fields were a green patchwork, interspersed with little hills and hazel nut groves . . . with rowan trees . . . with small farm cottages. The roads might have been called small brown lanes, but there was a leisurely perfection about them and a magic. They twisted and turned on themselves and went in any direction they chose. There was mischief in them. Were these like the little roads of Cloonagh? Sometimes, they took you into a man's haggard and when you thought to have to call at the cottage and apologize, they turned round and were out and away again . . . and my eyes had been closed to the loveliness of all this country. They had been closed to the kindness of its people. Maybe I had been poisoned by my own family, but all at once, I saw quite clearly that I had lived in paradise as a child, and never known it . . . and God had brought me home again . . .

Michael was 'the starting stick' for my new house. He and I would found it together, if only the starting stick held fast. He was the most important issue of my whole existence and I knew this as truth. I had had dreams of building a dynasty of white horses to rival the white horses of Mannanan McLir, that rode the Atlantic. It wanted maybe two good brood mares and a white stallion. We had it all in the palm of our hands with the legend of the Colleen Bawn. I sat on a bale of straw in the stable on the night of the second day with the lantern lit and swinging over my head and hoped that Michael would come out to me, but he did not come. I was lonely for him as I saw visions and dreamed dreams.

We had capital now. We had immense goodwill and people would back us. We just wanted a start and we could have the Colleen Bawn stables. We could get the spirit of Ireland with us . . . yet why did Michael not come out to talk to me, why did the Professor not reply to me? I knew what the answer would be. It had happened before. 'You must settle it for yourself, Sister Mark.'

He had no intention of writing to me to say 'Marry this honourable young man'. I must trust my own judgement, yet Michael seemed to have turned into a polite stranger . . . perfectly kind, with impeccable manners. There was no way of reaching him and it was my own fault. I had been niggardly with my trust, but had I?

Yet forty-eight hours was almost past . . . a period of time, I recognized well from intensive care. It could be over quickly, but mostly it passed, second by second . . . and now time had run slowly . . .

My thoughts ticked by with the seconds . . . is he or isn't he? Is he or isn't he? Is he or isn't he? Is he or isn't he?

Isn't he what? Is he a villainous murderer from the espionage personnel of some evil nation, where a man can be caught and his nails torn out? Always it came back to that. Were his nails torn out? Merciful heaven! I had seen them. I had dressed them, day after day. They might have been caught in machinery . . . They might have been . . . might have been . . . might have been . . .

The waiting time was almost over, but the last night was a hundred years. Then it was over, time to go to the stile to meet Michael and go with him up the cliff road, but it was only a small narrow lane, like the little roads of Cloonagh.

At least I had held off from throwing myself into his arms, and telling him that I loved him, no matter what he had done . . . that I never wanted to live without him . . . that he could have me on any terms he chose. I had told him I trusted him . . . right or wrong . . . no more . . . no less . . .

God help me! Maybe I regretted that I had not told him I loved him, but it was too late now, for the dawn was coming.

7

The Diagnosis

The morning was very new and the mist not quite risen from the fields when I reached the stile. He was there waiting for me and if God had told me that here was the Archangel Michael, at that moment, I might have believed him. I had had a suspicion of it all the time. Yet he was all seaman, the white high-necked sweater, the blue-black trews ... the line of beard along his chin, the buccaneer look to him. Almost I expected a gold ring in his ear and that was a far cry from a halo. I stood there as uncertain as ever I had been in my whole life and the prayer to St. Michael went like ticker tape through my head.

'Holy Michael, Archangel! Defend us in the day of battle. Be our safeguard against the wickedness and against the snares of the devil. May God rebuke him, we humbly pray, and do thou, Prince of the Heavenly Host, by the power of God, thrust down to hell, Satan, and all the wicked spirits, who wander through the world for the ruin of souls ... '

I stood there in dark sweater and jeans, with stout brogues on my feet against the dew of the morning and knew that this was a strange prayer to take possession of my soul at that particular moment of time.

His hand was out to greet me and his presence brought the first beam of the sun.

'Good day to you, Cordelia. May battle never start between thee and me.'

I might try to laugh at it, but my tension broke in a tide of words.

'There's no talk of battle ... never has been. You know well I trust you ... always have trusted you. If we've been caught up in some trap, let's get out of it, the best we can, I'm on your side, right or wrong.'

I walked on up the slope ahead and wondered what had made me make such a declaration. There was a deal to be settled up, before we could forget all that had been. It was just that the sun had shot its first beam across the land and I had known all was right for us. He drew level with me, took my hand in his and I thought that there was no escape for either of us in this world.

'I'm glad,' he said, and we walked on through the dewy machair and not a word between us.

I had accepted him in good faith and he was happy about that, very happy and I was happy too and the dew was washing the orchids to a carpet of semi-precious jewels. The sweet peppery smell of the gorse was all about us, getting stronger in the sun. The larks were singing higher and higher in the sky and now here was the mighty stretch of the Atlantic, that seemed to reach to the ends of the earth.

Then came the cliff plateau and some people already there, maybe half a score all told. My eye caught Guard Sheehan, but there was nobody else I knew and an elderly man was coming to meet us, a man in a dark suit, and he near enough to retiring age, with white hair and the square trustworthy face of a sailor, and he leaning on an ebony stick, for he limped a little.

'What are you people doing here? I thought the area had been closed off?'

Guard Sheehan had come across to say that I was the lady of the castle and there was talk that went to and fro and all very cordial and the 'Admiral of the Cinque Ports' as I thought of him was graciously giving his binoculars into my hands . . . and saying how sorry he was to try to order me off my own land.

'It should be interesting — er — Sister Mark. I hear that's what they call you. We're going to send a hand down the cliff presently.

It all seems proved conclusively . . . but . . . '

He took himself away after a polite interval and I pitied any poor sailor man who had to lower himself out over the fall of that cliff. They had all the gear ready. Just for now, they were scrutinizing the very edge at one point. They had found a place where it seemed there might have been a fresh fall. I glanced down at the sea and saw three ships, two frigates of Her Majesty's Navy, and one of them had what I took to be lifting gear on board . . . the same sort of thing that they used to load cars on cross channel ferries, or so my untutored brain told me. The Irish ship was smaller, but it was as lively as a terrier. It sailed about, and in and out and was obviously in command of its own waters.

There was a diver making ready to go down from one of the grey frigates. Through the glasses I could see him as closely, as if I stood by his side, as closely as I could see the young man, who was preparing to go down the cliff, not forty feet from where I stood on the edge. They concentrated on the recent fall. My skin crept with the terror, when I thought of lowering myself out over the tremendous depth and the older man was beside me, the one who had lent me his glasses.

'Maybe it might be wiser if you lay prone. I

confess that I'm worried about you going so near to danger in such a carefree manner.'

Little did he know, I thought, but I stretched myself out full length and kept his binoculars and he made no objection. Michael was squatting at my side. The sailor let himself spring out from the top, lowering himself and jouncing with his feet against the side of rock. There were men, who lowered him foot by foot and there was an expertise about them. Maybe I had the same expertise in 'intensive care' in the hospital. Maybe they would blanch if confronted with silence from a cardial monitor, and the last straight line of death. Maybe there was a job everybody could do 'special'.

'The bare black cliff clanged round him, as he based his feet on juts of slippery crags that rang, sharp smitten with the dint of armed heels', I thought, and that was Tennyson.

The elderly man was standing again behind where I lay.

'It's very kind of you to let us run wild about your land. It's just a routine matter . . . ends that must be tidied away. You'll realize the importance of this type of affair to the whole world. Maybe nobody has put you in the picture, but it all swings on the mineral rights of one very small nation.'

He knelt by my side, rather more

confidentially, though Michael at my other side, must have heard every word he said. Secrecy did not seem all that important. I thought fleetingly that perhaps they were trying to advertise something. We had headlines in the World Press for all I knew.

'This small nation has tremendous mineral rights, of a very special substance indeed. They have independence now and such power in their possession that they don't even know. It brings sharks around . . . two sharks actually, but you'll know all about it.'

I knew nothing about it at all. I just kept my mouth shut. That was always the way to hear more, but he had gone off to call to the man, who was down the cliff.

A thin voice crept up from below, as the man who was paying out the rope said in a mechanical voice, 'Fifty metres, sir.'

'Nothing to report down here,' came the echo from below. 'A fresh fall from the edge of a spur at about forty metres . . . nothing else.'

There was no point in going down any farther it seemed, and I sighed in relief and heard Michael take a deep breath, at my side. We were isolated from the others, just at that moment and like St. Paul on the road to Damascus, maybe I saw it all.

'There should have been blood, Michael

. . . and maybe the horn of nails on a ledge . . . there should have been microscopic pieces of skin, but not now. Thank God, not now.'

I handed him the glasses and he looked down at the cliff face and he was as white as wax under his tan.

'Should there? Should there indeed?' he asked me. '*Sister Mark.*'

The divers were going down into the sea far below. Here was something which might entertain millions on the television screens, but it did not interest me, only horrified me.

The picture was coming out of the unknown, as if it formed out of the mists of time, a piece here and a piece there. There was this nation, that had grown powerful, but not powerful enough to look after itself. There were two strong powers who wanted to engulf it and so world power might go into the wrong hands . . . here was intrigue at top level.

There was a car that had been sent over a cliff, but why? The United Nations were anxious to make it known that a certain gentleman was dead by accident, but he was dead by design.

The diver had disappeared under the grey waters and there was a long space where nothing happened, only an initial bubbling and then the smooth regular surging of the waves.

'There must have been blood on that cliff, Michael,' I said again and he turned his head towards me and said 'Yes'.

There were ledges with cutting edges . . . ledges with cutting edges, that could desecrate the hands of a desperate man . . . rocky places, that could flay his chest, juts on rock, that could deal out one sharp finishing blow to his temple.

There was no kindness and no mercy in this cliff. Had I not sought for mercy from here and not found it . . . but I had found it . . . suddenly I was shaken by the thought that maybe there had been a listener. Maybe he *had* sent down his archangel, Michael, to help me. I was stricken to a cessation of all thought by that idea, but the scene changed in front of the lenses of the glasses and the time went inexorably on. Hours had passed, but I was not conscious of time any longer . . . only of eternity.

I saw the small ledge not forty yards down. I saw the broken rowan tree, with the blossoms all dead. I thought of the berries, that would never come and that how if you crushed rowan berries, maybe in the fall of the year, they would turn to blood red. There was nothing there. I moved my sights up the cliff and saw the crannies and the juts, that might have been found by a desperate man's feet and hands . . . and how the edges of stone could have taken skin and finger nails and left a bleeding body, if ever he reached the top. He would have crucified himself against that cliff. I imagined he had done just that . . .

Down far below, there was a diver surfacing and he was winched on deck for a time and then went down again and now the crew of the derrick was in action with cables and all the things that meant lifting gear. What did I know of winching gear?

It came up out of the sea like a giant turtle, breaking the grey surface, this important car . . . not a Mini, not a Ford Escort. Here was a prestige car and even in her death, she kept the touch of grandeur in the long bonnet and the two flags on the chrome of the bumpers. She had been below the seas for a long time and she was done for, but she would not relinquish her pride, even though there were barnacles on her roof and seaweed that hung dripping ribbons from the smashed windows . . . even though one door hung from a single hinge.

'Number one staff car from this division. That's Captain Gatling's car. I know it well.'

The identification was made. I do not

know who made it, only heard the long sigh from Michael, as he saw the car, bashed, buckled, ruined and still flying its colours.

They brought it up on the derricks and I knew that Michael's lower lip was caught in his teeth. Now the cables were taking the strain and the car was free of the sea and being brought in gently to rest on the deck.

It swung round and poised itself and water rushed out from every crevice. The windows were shattered and jagged and still the trailing ribbons clung to it and cascaded out on the deck. There was a clutter of things that flowed out . . . perhaps the sodden papers of maps, cushions in fragments perhaps . . . perhaps . . . nothing else.

There was a walkie-talkie communication between cliff and sea. I heard the tiny voice, that chattered from somewhere behind me, but it was all a scene in a drama and maybe it had no part of my life, yet I knew well it had.

'Nothing unexpected down here, sir, I think between us, we have had confirmation of the accidental fall from the cliff. Death by misadventure, as we thought. We can pack up and go home, don't you think, sir?'

'Permission to weight anchor . . . sir?'

They went their ways, little by little. The two frigates were away to the east and the car with them lashed down on deck. There was etiquette between nations with some signalling between them and the Irish ship and then it was on its way too.

I sat up and grasped my elbows in my hands ... gave the officer back his glasses and thanked him, offered him the hospitality of Cormac's Castle and was glad when he thanked me politely, but said no.

They were all gone, but for Michael and myself and really, we had work and to spare down on the farm and no time to be gossiping idly on the cliff, but we knew that John Joe would see to what had to be done.

Here were matters of the utmost importance to decide. I stretched myself out again and looked down over the edge of the cliff. If he were a villain, now here was full opportunity to send me after Captain Gatling. I looked back again at that long climb up the cliff. The berries would never come again on that rowan tree, because it had spread its branches out to catch a human life. It was possible for a man with great courage and endurance to reach the top ... even if the lightning was flashing into his eyes and the rain lashing his back with whips. I half closed my eyes and I called up every bit of perception I possessed. The car had left the depot on a night 'that was as black as a dog's mouth', but maybe the turn to the cliff was deliberate. This was guessing . . . but perhaps it had been meant to happen. There was this talk of an emergent nation and two world powers, who were out to grab its assets . . . and another nation, or perhaps United Nations determined that it would not happen. It was far beyond my comprehension. Michael Gatling . . . Michael Gatling . . . Michael Gatling. Who was Michael Gatling? He was the pivot on which the whole operation swung. He had not been popular with sharks.

He had to be seen to die and that was what had happened. There had been a play on television a while back, a story from the last world war . . . where a dead man had been launched into the sea and that would explain it all. He had had documents planted on him, to be found. I had it now, as I remembered it, I said the words aloud . . .

'But I hae dreamed a dreary dream,
Beyond the Isle of Skye.
I saw a dead man win a fight
And I dreamed that man was I . . . '

I turned my head to look at Michael, sat up and clasped my knees with my hands and met his eyes squarely.

'Was Michael Gatling dead when you put

242

him into the sea in your car?' I asked him and that was a very long shot at the target.

He stood up and walked a bit away from me . . . came back to stand looking down at me, and I wondered if he would send me to my death for my skill in solving puzzles.

'It was a planned operation, very secret, very important,' he said. 'It's worked out. That's all that matters.'

'Oh, no, it's not,' I said fiercely. 'Have you no thought for me?'

'You said you trusted me. Just go on trusting me, though perhaps I'll never be able to explain it to you.'

I got to my feet and defied him, told him that he would explain it all straight away, or I'd turn on my heel and walk out of his life. It had been no easy thing for me to trust him, but I had trusted him and now he must trust me. I was not going to take every word he told me and put it in the *Cork Examiner* as front page news in tomorrow's edition and if he did not trust me now, I had no intention of ever marrying 'a pig in the poke'.

'I still don't like that expression,' he said and smiled and I knew well that here was no villain.

He took my hand in his and we walked down the hill towards the House of Jackdaws and I knew that in him, I had found my starting stick. Here was no false brittle piece of twig, that would break and go skittling down the chimney stack to end on a bare grey hearth.

'I was Michael Gatling. I had been built up to be Michael Gatling for a purpose, but there was no such a person as Michael Gatling. I was in charge of this business with the little nation, that seemed to have inherited the earth. They were all after it, like alligators after a carcase. I had carried the plot so far, but there was chance they would go on dealing with me. There were other men could do the end game, but I had to be seen to be dead . . . they would have no truck with me. They had me marked down for death anyway.'

It was impossible that such things could happen today, but I knew they happened. I knew he told the truth.

'The Mafia do that sort of thing!' I told him, and he smiled.

'We had to find a dead man that matched me in every particular. It did not matter to me if I was seen to be dead, for I had never been. I was Michael France and all I had to do was to step back into my own identity, only it did not work out that way.'

He stopped at the point, where there was the last view of the sea and turned round, turned me round with him and we looked out on the incomparable beauty of the golden path to the horizon.

You might think it possible to walk along it and come to Atlantis, but I knew that I was going to Atlantis in another direction. I turned back to where John James Benedict Cormac's Castle lay at our feet, but my castle now, caught in the rays of the setting sun with the mountains rising behind it in every colour of the spectrum. The clouds were shifting with the light wind and the colours were alive and moving across the face of the hills and the valleys . . . and the yellow gorse was ruler over it all, the little lambs, like puffs of wool . . . and soon there would be green pasture with white horses . . . and even now the primroses were hiding in every cranny — and the cowslips would come — and the wild roses.

Here lay Tir-nan-Oge, Brigadoon, Hy Brasil . . . and here we would live happily. I felt that maybe we walked through the field of the cloth of gold, for the way the orchids shone our feet.

'I took my own car that night and I drove it to the cliff . . . that car you saw just now. They had given me a passenger, but I didn't know who he was. I will never know . . . just somebody, who did a mighty important job

. . . a nobody who maybe kept nations from making war upon nations, but dead, quite dead. It was all so simple and it should have gone smoothly. Then perhaps God decided that it wasn't all that easy. After all, He is the Lord of Creation and he wanted the decision.'

He was far away from me now, back on the cliff top in the darkness . . . the storm breaking over his head, again.

I opened the door and got out and the lightning struck into my face. The door of the car took me over. I found myself on a ledge, held by a tree branch. The car went past me down the cliff, like a great fallen eagle. It dealt a blow to my temple and I clung there . . . then after a long time, I thought I might make a climb of it. It was an impossible cliff to climb, but nothing is impossible, if you pray hard enough. It's a funny thing, but I felt no pain, as I went up, didn't know there was anything wrong till you asked how my hands had got in such a state.'

He was back with me again, when he had been in another world.

'I was walking along the avenue of a house. You stood on the veranda. I thought I might not make the distance to the house. You were there, in a green velvet dress, and if I could get to you, somehow, I thought you'd help.

There was a party on in the house. I wanted to talk to you, but there were no words in my mouth. There was a man behind you and he thought I was drunk. Maybe I fell. It's not clear in my head, but somebody threw a blanket over me. I tried to say that I was not drunk, but I didn't know how I had got into such a state. Maybe I was drunk . . . for I had no recollection of who I was or why I was there. I was dressed in G.I. dress, but I thought that was not right. I had known what I was supposed to do. At one time, I had known, but it had all run out of my brain. There was a plan laid out to follow and I could not remember the first bit about it . . . but I knew, by some sort of instinct, that I must lie hid. That was the last bit of knowledge I had. On no account must anybody know where I was . . . '

I was back on the veranda again, remembering the man who had come in from nowhere. Maybe he had just climbed up forty metres of impossible cliff. I saw myself, my hand on his pulse, trying to decide, if he was drunk or if he was not. He had said his head hurt and he would like to lie down . . . but maybe he had to keep walking or he might die.

'I was supposed to die, wasn't I?' he had asked me and then he had pitched forward to lie at my feet and I had seen the tortured nails, the bloodied shirt, the head wound.

It all matched up now. I was almost quite sure of it . . . am almost quite sure of it, till this very day.

He was Michael France and they had taken his identity from him . . . built him up to be a top man in espionage . . . a man, who could disappear and be seen to be dead . . . a man, who could reappear on earth as Michael France, who had been a clever unit in espionage . . . a man, who was a chameleon, who could be built up to work on an international scale . . . and then fail, almost fail, because there were villains, who were afraid of his power. They would have him killed, so he was killed. His new identity was killed. There must be a handful of men such as he, capable of finding a successful outcome to bargaining, so there would be no more war. I did not understand it. I cared not much about it . . .

Here at our feet, lay my home and all the future laid out for it . . . and a new master, that had none of King Lear in him.

Here was a man, who could take command and turn this kingdom into happiness. Here was the starting stick that held and now there was no more to do, just put in other twigs and sticks and the nest would hold.

It was all going to run as it had been planned to run from the beginning . . .

We went on down the sheep path and the land was sweetly pretty.

'And to think I had the opinion now and again that you were the Archangel Michael, sent down from God to help me, because I had faced Him on the edge of that cliff. The evening before you fell from heaven, I faced Him and I demanded my rights. Maybe I got them?'

There was a letter back from 'the Proff', waiting on the hall table when I got home and maybe it helped me, but in my mind, I was still thinking of the pink tinge that life had taken as its right . . . of the little lanes, that twisted and turned, of the sun low in the sky, of the small hills, with the young lambs and the pastures, where in one year or two or three, white horses might roam, like creatures from another world, so full of grace and beauty . . . like horses of Mannanan McLir, who rode the seven seas, the perfection of it all.

I stood in the hall and slid a finger along the flap of 'the Proff's' letter, opened it. Here was his answer to all my problems.

'The King of France married Cordelia without a dowry,' it said. 'This is an honourable young man, in the present day warfare. At least be glad that you'll come to him with a dowry and we'll thank Cormac for that, only it was in no way essential. Here is a young man, who would go to battle against your foes. Marry him quickly and breed sons, for this nation has need of people like you and him. Breed white horses, if you must, for of such stuff are dreams made on . . . The world has grievous need of both . . . '

I put the letter down and turned to him and his arms were about me and the day was sparkling about us. Rose would be impatient for us in the kitchen and the fire burning brightly . . . with rashers and eggs ready to be slipped into the pan and that crusty home-made bread, that Guard Sheehan liked so much, with plenty of butter fresh from the churn and with blackberry jelly, made from the wild blackberries, and soon the blackberries would come again . . . and again.

It all went without saying. I would marry Michael France and we would have a happy fulfilled life. We would do the things that the Professor demanded of us and we might live in Tir-nan-Oge or Brigadoon . . . and the strange incident of Michael Gatling would be noted down in naval history, but always the little doubt lives in my mind. I remember that day on the cliff with the lightning flashing down on me and remember my cry against heaven. There is just a possibility . . . the remotest possibility, that He sent one of His great angels down. There's no proof that He did . . . equally no proof that He did not.

We have four sons now and a great many graceful white horses and still I look at him and always the same question tantalizes me. Did the Lord of Heaven send one of His great angels down? There's no possible proof that the man, who was swept over the cliff, was the same man that climbed up the crucifixion of those same cliffs and came along the avenue to find me. He has the look of an archangel about him, but surely he would not choose to remain below here on earth, on an Irish farm, raising white horses, that would match the white horses of Mannanan McLir, that ride the wild Atlantic . . .

'But you never know. There are more things in heaven and earth, Horatio, than are dreamt of in your philosophy . . . '

You never know . . .

This one small question teases me and teases me and will not let my mind run free. Was the man, that was swept down into the sea that night . . . the living man, the same man, that climbed up that impossible cliff face? I leave it to you . . .

We do hope that you have enjoyed reading this large print book.

Did you know that all of our titles are available for purchase?

We publish a wide range of high quality large print books including:
Romances, Mysteries, Classics
General Fiction
Non Fiction and Westerns

Special interest titles available in large print are:
The Little Oxford Dictionary
Music Book
Song Book
Hymn Book
Service Book

Also available from us courtesy of Oxford University Press:
Young Readers' Dictionary
(large print edition)
Young Readers' Thesaurus
(large print edition)

For further information or a free brochure, please contact us at:
Ulverscroft Large Print Books Ltd.,
The Green, Bradgate Road, Anstey,
Leicester, LE7 7FU, England.
Tel: (00 44) 0116 236 4325
Fax: (00 44) 0116 234 0205

Other titles in the
Ulverscroft Large Print Series:

STRANGER IN THE PLACE

Anne Doughty

Elizabeth Stewart, a Belfast student and only daughter of hardline Protestant parents, sets out on a study visit to the remote west coast of Ireland. Delighted as she is by the beauty of her new surroundings and the small community which welcomes her, she soon discovers she has more to learn than the details of the old country way of life. She comes to reappraise so much that is slighted and dismissed by her family — not least in regard to herself. But it is her relationship with a much older, Catholic man, Patrick Delargy, which compels her to decide what kind of life she really wants.

SLAUGHTER HORSE

Michael Maguire

The Turf Security Division is surprised and suspicious when playboy Wesley Falloway's second-rate horses develop overnight into winners. Simon Drake investigates, but suddenly there is a new twist — someone is out to steal General O'Hara, the star of British bloodstock, owned by Wesley Falloway's mother. With a few million pounds at stake, lives are cheap; Drake finds himself both hunter and quarry in a murderous chase where even his closest associates may be playing a double game.

MERMAID'S GROUND

Alice Marlow

It's been five years since Kate Williams' beloved husband died, leaving her with two young children to raise. Now she's built a good life in one of Wiltshire's prettiest villages, and she has her dream job, as gardener at Moxham Court. For the last year, Kate has had a lover, roguishly attractive Justin Spencer, but he won't commit to more than a night here and there. When she takes in a male lodger, Jem, Kate's secretly hoping his presence will provoke a jealous reaction in Justin. What she hasn't reckoned on is exactly how attractive Jem will turn out to be.

HOT POPPIES

Reggie Nadelson

A murder in New York's diamond district. A dead Chinese girl with a photograph in her pocket. A plastic bag of irradiated heroin in an empty apartment. A fire in a Chinatown sweatshop. The worst blizzard in New York's history. These events conspire to bring ex-cop Artie Cohen out of retirement and back into the obsessive world of murder and politics that nearly killed him. The terrifying plot uncoils first in New York — in Artie's own back yard — then in Hong Kong, where everything — and everyone — is for sale.